Rosemary rushed forward and greeted Shelby with a gentle hug. "You're here! Katy was worried about you. Your dad and Mr. Lambright took your things upstairs, and as soon they're down we'll—" She broke off, looking out the back door. She turned to Katy. "It's been a busy morning with visitors. Ben and Ruthie are here."

Gramma Ruthie and Grampa Ben had promised to come out and let Dad know what the doctor said about Aunt Rebecca. Dad would be eager to talk to them. Katy said, "I'll get Dad."

But Dad clattered down the stairs and into the kitchen before Katy took a step toward the stairway. He brushed past Katy and headed outside. Rosemary hurried after him, letting the screen door slam behind her. Katy started to ask the Nusses if they'd like something to drink, but the sound of someone crying carried through the screen door.

Katy looked outside. Dad held Gramma Ruthie in his arms and Grampa Ben stood close, patting Gramma on the shoulder. Rosemary had both hands over her mouth. Katy's heart leaped into her throat. *It's something bad. Something really, really bad.*

Other books in the Katy Lambright Series:

katy's
decision

KIM VOGEL SAWYER

KATY LAMBRIGHT SERIES

ZONDERVAN.com/
AUTHORTRACKER
follow your favorite authors

ZONDERVAN

Katy's Decision
Copyright © 2011 by Kim Vogel Sawyer

This title is also available as a Zondervan ebook.
Visit www.zondervan.com/ebooks.

Requests for information should be addressed to:
Zondervan, *Grand Rapids, Michigan* 49530

ISBN 978-0-310-72288-5

Published in association with Hartline Literary Agency, Pittsburgh, Pennsylvania 15235.

Cover design: Kris Nelson
Cover portrait photo: Mike Heath/Magnus Creative
Interior design: Carlos Eluterio Estrada, Greg Johnson/Textbook Perfect

Printed in the United States of America

12 13 14 15 16 17 18 /QG/ 22 21 20 19 18 17 16 15 14 13 12 11 10 9 8 7 6 5 4 3 2

*"To everything there is a season,
and a time to every purpose under the heaven: ...
a time to keep, and a time to cast away ..."*
Eccl. 3:1, 6

Chapter One

"Katy, if you don't stop pacing, you're going to wear a hole in the floor."

Katy paused in her trek between the back door and the kitchen window and sent her stepmother a sheepish look. "I suppose I'm a little eager for Shelby to get here."

Rosemary raised her fine eyebrows. The corners of her green eyes crinkled with a teasing grin. "I would never have guessed." She went back to wiping the kitchen table, washing away the smear of flour meant to keep the kneaded dough from sticking to the table. Before Rosemary married Dad, Katy always cleaned up the messes. It was nice to have someone else take over the sticky chore.

Katy leaned on the edge of the counter and nibbled her thumbnail. "I just have so many things planned for us, you know? Shelby loves horses, so we'll probably be out in the pasture a lot with Shadow and Saydee." Katy's mare had delivered a beautiful foal only two weeks earlier. Saydee was the prettiest filly Katy had ever seen. "And Annika is going to teach Shelby calligraphy, and Gramma Ruthie said she'd show her how to make a small quilted wall hanging, and of course we want to do lots of talking and laughing, like we always do."

Katy moved to the back door and searched the road. Where were they? "Reverend Nuss said they'd be here by nine. I wonder why they're so late."

Rosemary's laughter rang. "Honey, it's only ten minutes after nine!" She crossed to the door and gave Katy's shoulders a quick squeeze. "Haven't you ever heard that a watched pot never boils? Maybe it's also true that a watched road never produces a car."

Katy toyed with the ribbon dangling from her white mesh headcovering and giggled. She must look like a ninny, staring at the road and waiting for the Nuss's car to magically appear. But she couldn't help it. Her best friend from Salina High North would spend six weeks of the summer on Katy's dairy farm while Shelby's parents and brother were in Africa with a group from their church for a mission trip.

Shelby had planned to go to Africa too, but she fell playing softball a week ago and broke her ankle. It was a bad break, requiring surgery — she'd be in a cast and on crutches for a few months. Katy felt bad that her friend had to cancel her trip, but she wouldn't deny being excited. After spending her entire life as the only child in the house, having Shelby around would be almost like having a sister. The girls intended to make the most of the situation.

Katy peered out again. Only fields of unripe green wheat beneath a clear blue sky greeted her eyes. No puff of dust on the road indicated an approaching vehicle. She sighed. "Maybe the time would pass faster if I stayed busy ..." Any other weekday Katy would be working in her aunt's fabric store in Schellberg, but Aunt Rebecca had an early appointment in Salina today to get the results of some tests the doctor had run last week, so she'd closed the store for the morning. Katy was glad to be home to welcome Shelby, but it also meant she had nothing to occupy her at the moment.

"Good idea," Rosemary said. "I washed towels this morning, and they need to be hung. Why don't you take them out to the line?"

The clothesline stood behind a tall fence so people driving by wouldn't see their laundry blowing in the wind. The fence would keep Katy from seeing the road too. But even if she couldn't see the road, she'd hear a car pull into their yard. "All right."

She retrieved the basket from the little mudroom off the kitchen. When she bent over to lift the basket, the ribbon ties from her cap swung across her cheeks, tickling like a spider. She gave her chin a flick that sent the ribbons sailing over her shoulders, then she bumped the screen door open with her hip.

The midmorning sun beamed brightly, heating the top of Katy's head through her mesh cap. Her feet crunched on the gravel driveway, startling a cardinal from the thick lilac bushes beside the house. She watched it swoop over the barn and out of sight, smiling at the beauty of its bright red plumage against the blue backdrop of sky.

Katy made a mental note to check the bushes for the nest. A cardinal pair had chosen the lilac bushes for their home several years ago, and one of the best parts of summer was watching the birds return to build a new nest, lay their eggs, and nurture their young. And this year she'd get to share it with Shelby. *If she ever gets here . . .*

Her feet gave a little skip as she rounded the corner to the clothesline. She plopped the basket onto the ground and pulled out a damp towel. The sun bounced off the bright white towel, forcing Katy to squint. Between clipping towels to the line, she tipped her head and listened for an approaching car. The breeze whispered, birds twittered from treetops, and cows — released from the milking machine to mingle in the pasture next to the barn — offered an occasional *moo* of contentment. But she didn't hear car tires on gravel.

Katy hung the last towel, and Shelby's family still hadn't arrived. She carried the empty basket to the house, scuffing the toes of her tennis shoes against the ground. What was keeping Shelby? If Katy's family had a telephone, she could call Shelby on her little cell phone and ask what had happened. But Katy's Mennonite sect wasn't allowed to have telephones in their houses. According to Dad, the church elders intended to discuss permitting members to put phones in their barns, the way some other Mennonite or Amish communities allowed. But even if they offered permission tomorrow, it wouldn't help her find out what had happened to Shelby today.

Just as she reached the back stoop, the sound of a car's engine captured Katy's attention. She spun to face the driveway, eagerness speeding her pulse, but disappointment washed away the rush of excitement. Instead of the Nuss's van, Caleb Penner's sedan pulled into the yard. Katy frowned. What was Caleb doing back? He'd left less than an hour ago after helping Dad with the morning milking.

Maybe he forgot something—he can be so scatterbrained.

Katy knew she should be more charitable toward Caleb, but the boy wore on her nerves worse than anyone else she knew. He teased too much, and when he wasn't teasing he was flirting. She disliked the flirting even more than the teasing. Her best friend in Schellberg, Annika, had a crush on Caleb, which made it even worse. Sometimes it seemed like Caleb meant to stir up trouble between Katy and Annika.

Katy grabbed the door handle and started to enter the house, but Caleb rolled down his window and called her name. She sighed. It would be rude to pretend she hadn't heard him. Besides, he'd follow her into the house if she didn't talk to him in the yard. Maybe if she talked to him outside, he wouldn't stay very long. She dropped the basket onto the stoop and trotted to the sedan.

"What do you need, Caleb?" She hoped she didn't sound as irritated as she felt. She'd been working at treating Caleb the way she wanted to be treated, the way the Bible taught. She just wished he didn't make it so hard.

Caleb stuck his head out the window and looked around, his freckled forehead all puckered. "Isn't your friend here yet?"

The whole town of Schellberg knew the Lambrights were keeping a worldly girl for part of the summer. Some people outright disapproved, some people thought it was a kind gesture, and others were worried Shelby might have a negative influence on the young people in town. But Dad had given permission, and that was all that mattered to Katy.

Katy said, "Not yet. Why?"

Caleb propped his elbow on the armrest and grinned. "I have an idea. Well" — he made a face — "my mom had an idea. I wanted to tell both of you, but ..."

Katy waited for him to finish so she could return to the house, but he just sat there grinning like she should be able to read his mind. She resisted a sigh. "And the idea is ...?"

He gave a little jerk, as if jarring loose his thoughts. "You know how you want to train Shadow's foal to pull a buggy?"

Katy gritted her teeth. Did Dad have to talk to Caleb about everything? The two spent too much time together in the dairy barn. She needed to ask Dad not to share her plans with Caleb — she didn't like him knowing everything about her. "I hope to eventually, but not for a while yet. Saydee's too young."

He wrinkled his nose, crunching his freckles together. "I know — gotta wait 'til she's two. But my horse, Rocky, is buggy broke, and I've got that little two-wheeled cart." He paused again.

Would he ever get to the point? Katy inwardly prayed for patience. "So ...?"

"Mom thought, since your friend can't walk around much, maybe you'd like to borrow Rocky and the cart while she's here. You could practice your driving skills on Rocky — might help you when it's time to start training Saydee. It'll also give you and your friend a way to get around. You know, to visit Annika or ... or me." His cheeks blazed red, hiding the copper-colored freckles. "After all, I'm hosting that party Friday night. Figured you'd bring your friend, so ..." His voice drifted off again.

Katy nibbled her lower lip. As much as she hated to

admit it, she liked Caleb's idea. Or rather, his mother's idea. Having a buggy-broke horse and a cart for her use over the next weeks would be wonderful. She could even drive it into town to Aunt Rebecca's shop instead of having Dad take her. If only it weren't Caleb's horse and cart she'd be borrowing. He might see her as beholden to him. And he might want her to repay him by going to one of the community activities with him as his date. She nearly shuddered thinking about it.

She tipped her head, lowering her brows into a slight frown. "You're sure you wouldn't need to use the cart during the summer? I wouldn't want to inconvenience you." She hoped he'd read between her words and recognize she wasn't asking for the cart—he was offering it. Since it was his idea, she shouldn't have to pay him back in any way.

"Sure I'm sure." He patted the steering wheel. "I have my car, so I don't need the cart. I can bring it over tonight, if you'd like." He sounded eager.

"Let me ask Dad first," Katy said, "and make sure it's okay with him." She suspected Dad wouldn't mind. Although he always quit what he was doing to transport her to town or pick her up again, sometimes it wasn't convenient for him. He'd probably see the cart and horse as a real advantage. *And maybe*, her thoughts went on, *if he gets used to me having my own transportation, he'll consider getting me a car of my own.* "Hopefully he'll say yes."

"Okay. I gotta come back for milking this afternoon—he can let me know then. I'll bring 'em over tonight if he agrees."

"That sounds fine."

Caleb put his car in reverse and revved the engine. "See

you later, Katy." He backed up in a U, pointing the front toward the road. Then he spun his tires to take off. Dirt billowed behind the car as he whizzed down the driveway.

Katy stumbled backward, waving her hands in front of her face to keep from breathing in the dust. Even so, her nose filled, and she coughed. Oh, that Caleb! He'd stirred up all that dust on purpose just to annoy her!

Dad stepped out of the barn, frowning after Caleb. "What's with that boy? He'll ruin his tires pulling stunts like that."

Katy coughed again then trotted to Dad's side. "Oh, you know Caleb ... he likes to show off."

"Well, I hope *you* never do things like that when you're driving."

Katy gawked at Dad. "Of course not!" To steer the conversation elsewhere, she told Dad about Caleb offering the use of his horse and cart. Dad listened, his lips pursed like they always were when he was thinking. When Katy finished explaining the benefits of having the cart for her and Shelby's use, he pushed his bill cap back and scratched his head.

"I don't know, Katy. It might be nice to have a buggy-broke horse and a cart around for you girls this summer, but what about feeding the horse? Are you supposed to take care of it while it's here?"

Katy hadn't thought about taking care of the horse — just using it. But she didn't see a problem. "I already feed and water Shadow and Saydee every day. It won't take much more time to take care of Rocky too."

"But it'll take more feed," Dad said. He slipped his hands in his trouser pockets. "Do you have money for extra oats and hay?"

Katy earned money by working in Aunt Rebecca's store, so she had more than enough to cover extra feed. But she preferred to use her money on other things, like fabric, books, or trips to the skating rink or bowling alley in Salina. And if the elders approved the use of telephones, she might see about buying a little cell phone similar to the one Shelby used. "Yes, I could cover it." She shrugged. "It'll only be for a few weeks — while Shelby's here. What do you think?"

Dad opened his mouth to answer, but the sound of a car engine interrupted him. They both looked toward the road. A white van — the Nuss's van — pulled into the drive. Katy waved her hand over her head in greeting and darted forward to meet the vehicle. Dad followed on her heels.

Reverend Nuss shut off the engine and opened his door. He held out his hand to Dad and bounced a grin in Katy's direction. "Hello, Samuel — Kathleen. I'm sorry we're so late."

Shelby's younger brother shot out of the backseat while Mrs. Nuss walked around the front of the van to join Katy and her dad. She gave Katy a quick hug and then left her arm around Katy's shoulders. "We took Jewel to her mother's place this morning, and our good-bye took longer than we'd expected. I think she was sad to see us go."

Katy marveled at the woman's explanation. Their foster daughter, Jewel, had spent so much time complaining about the rules at the Nuss house, Katy couldn't imagine her not celebrating being back with her mother again. "So Jewel isn't going to live with you anymore?"

Mrs. Nuss said, "It's a trial, so to speak, to see if her mother is able to care for Jewel again." She squeezed

Katy's shoulders before moving to her husband's side.
"We're praying it works out, for both of their sakes."

Katy nodded. "I'll pray for that too." Katy's mother had
died when she was young, but if she was alive, Katy would
want to spend time with her. Jewel was lucky to still have
a mom.

"Katy!" Shelby called from inside the van.

"Excuse me," Katy said. She dashed to the side door
and opened it. "Hey! You're here!"

Shelby stuck out her foot, which sported a thick white
cast wrapped in royal-blue tape. "We're both here." She
wriggled her toes, her pink polish glinting in the sunlight.
"Are you ready for us?"

Katy laughed. "Sure am!"

Mr. Nuss pulled Shelby's suitcases — all three of them —
from the back of the van, and he and Dad carried them to
the house. Katy and Shelby followed slowly, with Shelby
leaning on her crutches. Katy told her about the possibility
of using Caleb's horse and cart, and Shelby's face lit with
delight. Katy couldn't stop smiling. Shelby never made fun
of the simpler way Katy lived or acted like she thought Katy
was weird. Katy appreciated Shelby's acceptance. They were
going to have so much fun over the next several weeks.

When they reached the stoop, Mrs. Nuss showed Katy
how to help Shelby navigate stairs. Since the bedrooms
were all upstairs in their farmhouse, Katy would be helping Shelby a lot. Katy held her breath while Shelby wob-
bled on the concrete step then let it out in a whoosh when
Shelby stepped safely into the house.

Rosemary rushed forward and greeted Shelby with a
gentle hug. "You're here! Katy was worried about you.

Your dad and Mr. Lambright took your things upstairs, and as soon as they're down we'll — " She broke off, looking out the back door. She turned to Katy. "It's been a busy morning with visitors. Ben and Ruthie are here."

Gramma Ruthie and Grampa Ben had promised to come out and let Dad know what the doctor said about Aunt Rebecca. Dad would be eager to talk to them. Katy said, "I'll get Dad."

But Dad clattered down the stairs and into the kitchen before Katy took a step toward the stairway. He brushed past Katy and headed outside. Rosemary hurried after him, letting the screen door slam behind her. Katy started to ask the Nusses if they'd like something to drink, but the sound of someone crying carried through the screen door.

Katy looked outside. Dad held Gramma Ruthie in his arms and Grampa Ben stood close, patting Gramma on the shoulder. Rosemary had both hands over her mouth. Katy's heart leaped into her throat. *It's something bad. Something really, really bad.*

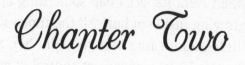

Chapter Two

Katy remembered to say "Excuse me" to her guests before racing outside to join her family. She arrived in time to hear Grampa Ben say, "She'll start treatment right away."

Katy tugged Rosemary's sleeve. "What is it? What's wrong with Aunt Rebecca?"

Rosemary slipped her arm around Katy's shoulders. "She has cancer, honey."

Katy's knees buckled. She stared into her stepmother's concerned face, her heart pounding so hard she feared it might explode. Cancer? But cancer killed people. Aunt Rebecca couldn't possibly have cancer.

Dad turned Gramma Ruthie toward the house. "Let's go inside—out of the sun. Katy, make a fresh pot of coffee."

Shelby's brother ran outside to play, but Reverend and Mrs. Nuss joined Dad, Gramma Ruthie, and Grampa Ben in the front room. Shelby sat at the kitchen table while Rosemary sliced banana nut bread and Katy prepared a pot of coffee. Her hands shook, but she ground the beans, filled the aluminum percolating basket, and poured water into the pot. How could she work so calmly, fixing coffee and arranging mugs on a tray like it was any other gathering, when Aunt Rebecca had something ugly and dangerous growing inside of her? All the times she'd gotten annoyed with her aunt came back to haunt her, and she vowed she'd never let frustration get control of her again if only Aunt Rebecca would be all right.

Shelby propped her chin in her hand. She looked worried. "Maybe I shouldn't stay this summer if . . ."

Rosemary crossed to the table and gave Shelby's shoulder a squeeze. "Oh, no. I think God knew Katy would need a friend this summer." She looked at Katy with a sad smile. "Am I right? Having Shelby here is a blessing."

Katy nodded. As much as she loved her friend Annika, Annika tended to be gloom and doom about things. Shelby was more positive. "And maybe you can help out at the fabric store with me." She glanced at Shelby's thick cast. "You could sit at the counter and run the cash register."

"I'd be glad to help," Shelby said.

Katy and Rosemary carried the banana bread and coffee to the front room, and the grown-ups discussed Aunt Rebecca's diagnosis. Although Katy enjoyed adding new words to her vocabulary, she resented adding *tumors*, *radiation*, and *chemotherapy* to her word bank. Those were words she'd rather never know.

Grampa Ben finished, "The doctor said they caught it early, and she should be all right. But it will be a rough few months while she goes through treatment."

A single tear trailed down Gramma Ruthie's cheek. "I plan to stay with Albert and Rebecca to help out with the children." She turned a wobbly smile on Katy. "And I'm so glad our Katy is familiar with the store. She can keep things going there so Rebecca doesn't need to worry."

Katy nodded eagerly. "Shelby said she'd help too. Maybe even Annika would come in if we need some extra hands so Aunt Rebecca can rest."

Grampa Ben chuckled. "If I know Rebecca, she'll want to be at the store whether she feels up to it or not. But she'll have to go to Salina for her treatments, so there will be plenty of days she'll be relying on you, Katy-girl. Thank you for being willing to take over."

Being in full charge of the fabric shop would be very different from following Aunt Rebecca's directions. For a moment, Katy felt panic trying to take hold. She recited Philippians 4:13 inside her head: *I can do all things through Christ which strengtheneth me.* The verse — one of Aunt Rebecca's favorites — calmed her. She said, "I'm glad to do it." Even though she'd hoped for lots of free time to have fun with Shelby, she discovered she was happy to help her family.

Reverend Nuss cleared his throat. "We're going to need to get on the road soon, but before we go, may I pray with you?"

Dad offered a solemn nod. "We would appreciate your prayers, Brother Tim."

Everyone bowed their heads and Shelby's dad began to pray. Katy couldn't help peeking around the circle while he asked God to bring healing to Aunt Rebecca and strength and peace to the family. She examined a variety of contrasts — Rosemary's white cap against Mrs. Nuss's uncovered, shoulder-length hair; Dad's button-up chambray work shirt and tan trousers against Reverend Nuss's polo shirt and knee-length plaid shorts; Grampa Ben's and Gramma Ruthie's wrinkled, vein-lined hands against

Shelby's smooth skin ... For some reason, the pictures put a lump in her throat. She closed her eyes as Reverend Nuss brought his prayer to a close.

"Finally, Lord, we praise You because we know You are a God who wastes nothing. You will use this experience to grow the Lambright family closer to each other and to You. Thank You for giving us all we need to face the challenges of this life. Amen."

"Amen," Dad and Grampa Ben echoed.

Shelby said good-bye to her family in the yard before they drove away. Grampa Ben and Gramma Ruthie left too, after receiving hugs from Katy and Rosemary. Dad and Rosemary wandered back to the house, their arms around one another's waists, and Katy and Shelby were left standing in the middle of the driveway.

Katy sighed. "This isn't exactly the way I had things planned."

Shelby bumped Katy with her elbow. "Aww, it's all right. We were gonna be kind of stuck anyway." She bobbed her cast-covered foot in the air then leaned more heavily on her crutches. "I sure feel bad for your aunt, though. It's got to be scary."

Katy nodded. Aunt Rebecca ran her store the way she wanted, bossed around her kids and husband, and advised everybody whether they wanted advice or not. She was always in control of everything. But she couldn't control cancer. Nobody could. And if it could happen to Aunt Rebecca, who'd never smoked or drank alcohol or ate junk food or any of the other things the biology teacher at Salina High North said could cause cancer, then it could happen to anyone. The sun beamed hot enough to roast Katy's head, but a shiver crept up her spine.

She admitted, "It scares me."

Shelby bumped Katy's elbow again, offering a sympathetic smile. "Well, let's —"

Dad called from the back door. "Katy? You and Shelby come eat an early lunch, and then I'll drive you into town. I'm sure Rebecca will open the store this afternoon, and she'll need to talk to you about the change in your duties over the next weeks."

❖

Usually Tuesdays were slow at the fabric shop, but the little bell hanging above the door rang all afternoon. People didn't come in to buy fabric, though. They came to see Aunt Rebecca. Over and over, Aunt Rebecca repeated what she'd heard from the doctor — "I have a marble-sized tumor. They'll do radiation to shrink it, then they'll surgically remove it, and finally I'll undergo chemotherapy to make sure the cells don't spread anywhere else in my body."

Katy marveled that Aunt Rebecca could share the news so calmly. Shelby even said, "Your aunt is amazing. She must have incredible strength!" Aunt Rebecca had always preached to Katy about finding strength in the Lord, but Katy had never seen it exhibited as clearly as on that Tuesday afternoon with Aunt Rebecca assuring the townspeople she'd be just fine, thanking them for their concern, and agreeing to let them know if she needed anything.

At five o'clock Aunt Rebecca turned over the little sign on the door to indicate the store was closed then sank into the chair beside her sewing machine and released a big sigh. She tucked a few stray hairs beneath her cap and sent the girls a tired smile. "For someone who did very little work today, I'm exhausted."

Katy found herself tongue-tied. She had no idea what to say to her aunt. She also found herself wanting to stare at the place where the tumor resided. So she shifted her gaze to her own linked hands in her lap.

Shelby said, "Emotional exhaustion is worse than physical exhaustion, I think."

"You're very right," Aunt Rebecca said.

Shelby wriggled on the stool behind the counter. "I'm curious about something ... You don't have telephones in Schellberg except for the one in the grocery store that everybody uses, right?"

Both Katy and Aunt Rebecca nodded.

"Then how did people find out already? I mean, it's like the whole town already knows, but you only found out this morning."

Aunt Rebecca laughed softly. "For one thing, Schellberg is a very small town, so it doesn't take long for news — whether good or bad — to spread."

Katy inwardly agreed. She loved little Schellberg, but often she wished she could keep things to herself. Sometimes a person preferred privacy.

Aunt Rebecca went on. "Everyone knew I'd had a biopsy a week ago — it was announced during Sunday worship so people could pray. The elder also announced that I would get my results this morning. So of course they'd want to know what the doctor said."

"When do you have your first radiation treatment?"
Shelby asked.

"Thursday morning."

Katy looked up in surprise. "So soon?"

"Well, we can't put it off, Katy." Aunt Rebecca's tone
turned tart.

"I—I suppose not." The lump returned to Katy's throat.

Aunt Rebecca went on matter-of-factly. "I'll have radiation five days a week, for three weeks. They want to
shrink it as much as they can before they do surgery."

"So they're not gonna ... you know ..." Shelby bit down
on her lower lip for a moment. "Cut off your breast?"

Shelby's straightforwardness made Katy cringe, but at
the same time she was glad her friend asked the questions
she didn't have the nerve to ask.

For a moment Aunt Rebecca sat in silence. Then
she drew in a breath and said, "We're trying to avoid a
mastectomy."

Mastectomy ... Another word Katy would rather not
know.

"The doctor believes the tumor is contained, and we
caught it early. Hopefully a lumpectomy will be enough."

How could Aunt Rebecca speak so calmly? The subject
made Katy's stomach churn. She swallowed. "So you'll
be gone every morning. What about afternoons? Will the
radiation make you too sick to come in?"

Aunt Rebecca propped her hands on her knees and
straightened her shoulders. "I'm not sure, Katy. Everyone
responds differently to treatment, but I suppose time will
tell. I hope to be in at least half the day so you won't have

to carry such a heavy load. But just in case, come here."
She rose and crossed to the counter.

Katy jumped up from her perch on the windowsill and
joined her aunt. For the next half hour, she listened as
Aunt Rebecca showed her how to record sales, returns,
and damaged items in the Sale and Inventory journals. It
didn't look too complicated. Katy thought she could handle
the recording.

"I'll plan on placing any necessary orders—it would be
too hard to explain how to determine amounts of supplies
to order." Aunt Rebecca closed the books and returned
them to the shelf under the counter. "I know you're familiar with organizing the shelves, cutting fabrics, and running the cash register, so there's no sense in us discussing
those responsibilities."

"Shelby said she'd operate the cash register, if you'd
like," Katy said. "She's really good at math."

Aunt Rebecca flashed Shelby a quick smile. "That's very
kind of you, Shelby—especially since you're supposed to
be on a vacation of sorts." She patted Katy's hand. "I know
you'll take good care of the store, Katy. I'm not worried at
all."

Katy appreciated her aunt's words, but she wondered
if Aunt Rebecca hadn't told a little fib. Worry lingered in
her eyes. "We'll"—she waved a hand in Shelby's direction
to include her—"pray you won't feel too sick so you can
come in as much as you want. I know you'd rather take
care of things yourself than trust it all to me."

Aunt Rebecca laughed—a genuine laugh. "You're right,
Katy. I do like to be in charge. But maybe ..." Her gaze

drifted off to the side. "Maybe it will be good for me to have to let go a little bit."

Someone pounded on the door. Katy jumped.

Aunt Rebecca frowned. "What is Caleb Penner doing here?" She hurried to the door and twisted the lock. The moment she opened the door, Caleb stepped through. "Caleb, we've closed for the day."

Caleb snatched his blue bill cap from his head. His hair stood up in reddish spikes. "Oh, I know. I'm not here to buy nothin'. Mr. Lambright asked me to pick up Katy and Shelby." His eyes bounced between the two girls then landed on Katy and stayed. "You ready to go?"

Katy looked at Aunt Rebecca. "Do you need me to do anything else?"

"Just be here tomorrow so we can open at nine, as usual," Aunt Rebecca said. "I'll plan on sitting back and letting you run things as a practice for when I won't be here."

"Let's go then." Caleb spun and charged out the door.

Shelby planted her crutches in her armpits and hobbled after Caleb. Katy followed, staying close to Aunt Rebecca. There were so many things she wanted to say—*Don't worry; you'll be all right; I'm sorry for the times I got angry at you*—but none of the things found their way out of her mouth. "We'll see you tomorrow."

Aunt Rebecca briefly touched Katy's cheek—a rare, affectionate gesture that made Katy want to cry. "Tomorrow," she said.

Katy gave her aunt a quick, almost desperate, hug. Then she dashed out the door.

Chapter Three

To Katy's surprise, Caleb's horse and green-painted, two-wheeled cart waited at the curb. Caleb stood beside the horse, grinning his familiar freckle-faced grin.

Caleb patted Rocky's muscled neck. "Your dad said Mrs. Lambright would help with the milking tonight so I could bring you the cart. I'm gonna let you drive to my place and drop me off, and then you can take it on home. It'll give you a chance to practice driving while I'm with you. That way, if you mess up, I can help you before you take over the cart by yourself."

Even though Aunt Rebecca had said basically the same thing about letting Katy run the store under her supervision tomorrow, Caleb's statement rankled. Katy put her hands on her hips. "I'm not an idiot, Caleb. And I've driven a cart before. Uncle Albert has one too, you know."

Caleb shrugged, still grinning. "Yeah, but your uncle's cart is four-wheeled, not two. And it's a lot bigger. The balance is different. His horse isn't as young and spirited as Rocky, either."

Katy pressed her lips together. Arguing with Caleb was

a waste of time. Besides, he was right—she'd never driven a two-wheeled cart before. Maybe it was best he was here to offer advice.

"Hop in," Caleb said. Then he looked at Shelby, who stood waiting at the curb. He grimaced, reaching up to tug at the brim of his bill cap. "Do you … need help?" He sounded scared she'd say yes.

Shelby's lips twitched, and Katy knew she battled a giggle. "Guess I better figure out how to get in by myself, because you don't come with the cart, right?"

Caleb's face turned bright red. He jerked the hat brim so low he nearly covered his eyes. "Um, no, not exactly."

Thank goodness. If Caleb came with the cart, Katy wouldn't borrow it. She bustled to Shelby's side. "I'll give you a hand."

"Thanks." With Katy's help, Shelby managed to heave herself over the edge of the cart. She collapsed into the leather-upholstered seat with a breathy laugh then swiped her hand across her forehead. "Phew! That was harder than I thought, but I'm aboard! Your turn."

Katy wedged Shelby's crutches into the narrow space below the seat then scrambled up with no trouble at all. But she and Shelby nearly filled the seat by themselves, and they still needed to make room for Caleb. Because the cart was essentially a springed seat mounted on a wood-wheeled frame, there wasn't even a tiny bed on the back for Caleb to sit in.

Shelby shifted to the very edge of the seat, and Katy scooted as close to Shelby as she could without sitting on her lap. "Well, come on, Caleb." She tried not to sound too grumpy.

His face still blazing, Caleb wriggled his hips into the narrow slice of seat remaining. The seat springs complained with the added weight. His shoulder wedged against Katy's, pinning her arm to her side. He grunted, jerked his arm into the air, and flung it behind Katy, nearly clunking her on the side of her head with his elbow. He laid his arm across the back of the seat, and even though it made them fit better, she didn't like the feel of his arm against her spine. She sat forward a bit to avoid contact and picked up the traces.

She sent a quick peek at Shelby. "You ready?"

Shelby clamped her hands on the seat's side edge. "Yeah. But don't hit any big bumps, or I might bounce off of here!"

Caleb laughed, the sound loud in Katy's ear.

Katy clicked her tongue on her teeth and gave the traces a steady pull. Rocky obediently backed the cart from the curb. Then Katy flicked the reins, and Rocky moved forward, drawing the cart into the street.

Caleb grinned, bumping Katy's shoulder with his wrist. "Good job. You're doin' great. So far."

Katy resisted rolling her eyes and guided Rocky to the edge of town. She kept Rocky to a gentle trot even though she wished she could hurry him to shorten the time in Caleb's presence. But she had to admit, Caleb wasn't being too much of a pain at the moment. He propped one boot on the cart's edge, giving her a little more room for her feet. She sensed he was as uncomfortable with their close seating arrangement as she was, which softened her toward him a bit.

For the first half mile or so, Caleb offered simple suggestions. Katy grated at receiving instruction from Caleb

Penner, but she kept quiet and let him talk. She wasn't familiar with Rocky, and she needed to know how to handle the big horse. Fortunately, Rocky was used to the cart. He didn't shy away from passing cars, just kept a steady *clop-clop* that stirred dust from the road. They reached the turnoff for Caleb's house, and Rocky pulled the cart around the corner without any prompting from Katy.

Caleb sat straight up, bopping Katy with his arm. "Don't let him do that." He took the reins from Katy's hands and pulled back on them. "Whoa ..." Rocky stopped, tossing his head and snorting in protest. Caleb frowned at Katy. "Make him back up and drive to the next mile marker. Then turn him and backtrack to my place."

But that would leave them in Caleb's company even longer. Katy was sweaty, tired, and ready to go home. "But—"

"You have to be in charge." Caleb slapped the reins into Katy's hands. "Make him follow your directions—don't follow his—or you'll end up where you don't want to be."

Katy sighed. As much as she hated to admit it, Caleb was right. If she was going to lead Rocky, she needed to establish her authority early on. With tugs on the reins and several teeth-clicks, she convinced the horse to reverse enough to return to the east-west dirt road. They started off again.

"Crazy horse," Caleb muttered, settling into the seat again with his arm behind Katy. "He's got a mind of his own."

Shelby leaned forward slightly and looked at Caleb. "Will he try to escape Katy's corral and run home every time we get him out?"

Caleb puffed up importantly. "He might, but that's why

I want Katy to make him mind. That'll let him know she's his boss." He tapped her shoulder again. "At least, for now."

Katy angled her shoulder forward to avoid his hand.

"When you girls come to my party on Friday, he might get confused," Caleb went on. "You'll prob'ly wanna get him out quite a bit—drive him up and down the roads and then back to your place just for practice so he knows he's supposed to be with you."

Shelby looked at Katy. "We're going to a party?"

Katy shrugged. "I'm—"

Caleb grinned. "Yeah! A singing and—"

"I'm not sure." Katy cut short Caleb's statement. "It'll depend on how Aunt Rebecca's doing." She gave the reins a tug, guiding Rocky to turn north. "If she can't be at the store at all, I'll have more responsibility there. I probably won't have time to go to parties." Katy felt a little guilty using Aunt Rebecca as an excuse, but she wasn't certain she wanted to attend Caleb's party. Especially with Shelby along. It might be awkward. "As for your suggestion, Caleb, about driving to help Rocky figure out where he's supposed to be right now, we'll get plenty of driving in, taking the cart to Aunt Rebecca's shop each day."

Caleb scrunched his lips to the side for a moment and stared at Katy. His intense scrutiny made her ears go hot. Finally he said, "I'm sorry. About your aunt, I mean. It's gotta be rough, knowing she's got something like cancer."

Just hearing the word spoken out loud sent Katy's stomach into whirls of nausea. She swallowed and didn't answer.

"Mom's gonna go check on her, see if there's anything

she can do to help ... with the kids and the house and stuff." Caleb nudged Katy again, but this time she didn't pull away. "If there's anything I can do ... you know, like mow their yard or something, would you let me know?"

Katy stared at Rocky's swishing tail while tears stung her eyes. Caleb had never been so nice. "S-sure, Caleb. Thanks." Rocky snorted, alerting Katy they'd reached Caleb's lane. She slowed Rocky and guided him on the curve that led to the house. The crunch of the wheels seemed loud in her ears as she drew the horse to a stop right outside Caleb's back door. She forced a smile. "Well, here you are."

"Yeah." But Caleb didn't hop down. His arm rested against Katy's back, warm and somehow comforting. "Rocky'll be fine. You handled him real good, Katy."

Real well, Katy's thoughts corrected, but not in an unkind way. "Thanks."

And still Caleb didn't get down.

The back door squeaked open and Mrs. Penner stepped out. Her freckled face, usually wreathed with a smile, looked serious. She stepped to the edge of the cart and reached across Shelby to cup Katy's hand with her soft fingers. "Katy, I heard about Rebecca. I'm so sorry."

Katy nodded. Would cancer now be the subject of every conversation? If so, Katy wasn't sure how she'd handle it. It was such an *ugly* word.

"Please let her know she's in my prayers. I intend to take a meal over Thursday so she won't have to cook after her first treatment."

Katy nodded again, but her voice seemed to have escaped her.

Mrs. Penner shifted her attention to Shelby. A soft smile curved her lips. "You must be Katy's friend from Salina. I'm Caleb's mother."

"I'm Shelby Nuss. It's nice to meet you," Shelby said.

"I'm sure Katy is glad to have you here, Shelby—you'll provide a needed distraction."

Shelby flicked a grin at Katy. "I hope so."

Mrs. Penner gave Katy's hand a quick squeeze and stepped back. "Caleb, come on in now and get your supper." She waved at the girls then disappeared into the house.

Caleb slowly removed his arm from the back of the seat. His fingers brushed across Katy's shoulders. Little shivers traveled down her arms to her fingers, and she tightened her grip on the reins. He climbed down then stood looking at Katy with a sad yet tender expression in his pale green-blue eyes. "Enjoy the cart now, Katy." He shoved his hands into his pockets and scuffed to the back porch. Before stepping inside, he sent one more look toward the cart—a look Katy couldn't quite decipher.

The moment the door closed behind him, Shelby said, "You know, he's a little geeky, but he's kind of nice too."

Katy gave the reins a snap, setting Rocky in motion. She didn't answer Shelby, though. Caleb *had* been nice. And somehow the nice Caleb bothered her more than the teasing Caleb. But she didn't know why.

Chapter Four

During the first days of Aunt Rebecca's radiation treatments, Katy and Shelby developed a routine that worked well for them. After Katy opened the shop, Shelby took up residence on a tall stool behind the cash register counter. Katy had showed her how to record the purchases and returns, so Shelby took over the bookwork and money exchanging while Katy cut fabric, straightened the shelves after shoppers rearranged items, and did the cleanup at the end of the day. Rocky dozed peacefully in a patch of grass behind the fabric shop, seemingly content with his new surroundings.

Aunt Rebecca came in each afternoon — sometimes for the entire afternoon, sometimes for only an hour or so — but it seemed to make her feel better to check in on the girls. So even though Katy believed they could handle the shop alone, she didn't begrudge Aunt Rebecca's visits. But seeing her aunt change day by day as the treatments robbed her of energy and appetite made Katy's heart ache, and as the days slipped by, Katy found herself wishing Aunt Rebecca would just go home after her treatments so she wouldn't have to witness their effect. Guilt for her self-ish reaction nearly tied her stomach into knots.

On the second Friday of Aunt Rebecca's radiation treat-ments — her seventh treatment — she entered the shop shortly after two o'clock, sank into a chair, and said wea-rily, "Katy-girl, come here, please. I need to talk with you."

Her heart pounding, Katy shot a quick glance at Shelby. Shelby's fearful expression did little to encourage Katy. She gulped and scurried to Aunt Rebecca's side. "Yes?"

A wobbly smile formed on Aunt Rebecca's lips. "I have good news. The tumor is shrinking much faster than ex-pected. An answer to prayer, yes?"

Katy nodded so hard her ribbons bounced on her cheeks. Every night, Dad prayed for healing for Aunt Rebecca, as did Katy and Shelby. She was certain most of the residents in Schellberg added their prayers as well. The tumor shrinking was wonderful news, and Katy wanted to celebrate it. But her aunt's nervous demeanor held her happy exclamation inside.

"What this means is my surgery has been moved up. I'll go into the hospital first thing Monday morning. They expect to keep me for a couple of days to let me heal and gain a little strength, and then ..." Aunt Rebecca blinked rapidly, removing a shimmer of tears from her dark eyes. "The chemotherapy starts."

Suddenly Katy understood Aunt Rebecca's sober reac-tion. According to Gramma Ruthie, chemotherapy was much harder to bear than radiation. Radiation only targeted one small spot — the site of the tumor — but chemotherapy would go into Aunt Rebecca's bloodstream, affecting her entire body. Katy hugged herself. "Oh." She didn't know what else to say.

Shelby pushed off the stool and limped around the counter, leaning on her crutches. She stood beside Katy, looking at Aunt Rebecca with sympathy glowing in her eyes. But she didn't say anything either.

Aunt Rebecca fiddled with a crease in her skirt as she continued. "I'm not sure what to expect. I still hope to come in part of the day. I'll only have chemotherapy once a week, you know. But ..." She lifted her head and met Katy's gaze. "I'm so sorry, Katy. I know you didn't expect to spend your entire summer in the store. Especially with your friend here." Her gaze shifted to include Shelby. "I understand you didn't even go to the Penners' party last week. I hope that wasn't because you were too tired from working here."

Apparently Katy's cousins, Lori and Lola, had told Aunt Rebecca Katy hadn't shown up at Caleb's party. Those two loved to tattle. She quickly assured her aunt, "We weren't too tired. But after checking on Shadow and Saydee" — that's all Katy had time to do ... check on the horses rather than play with Saydee or ride Shadow — "Shelby and I just decided to stay home. That's all."

Aunt Rebecca nodded slowly, but she didn't look as though she believed Katy. "Well, I'm sending you home early today so you'll be able to go to the party at Annika's this evening. I know she'll want you to come, and I don't want to spoil your entire summer. Once I start chemo, I have no idea how much more I'll depend on you. So grab some fun while you can, will you?"

Tears burned behind Katy's nose. Not once in all of her seventeen years had her aunt told her to have fun. In fact, the bossy, brusque, all-business aunt Katy had always known seemed to have disappeared. Receiving such frivolous instructions should have made her happy — hadn't she always wished Aunt Rebecca would be more softhearted? — but instead it scared her. She clutched her hands together. "Are you sure? We can stay. We don't mind."

Shelby added, "We don't mind at all."

Aunt Rebecca propped her hands on her knees and rose. She shook her head. "No, I want you to go on home. I'm going to start closing the shop at noon on Saturdays until I've finished all of my treatments, so you'll have a little free time on the weekends." She pushed the door open and raised one eyebrow. "Now scoot."

Katy and Shelby exchanged uncertain glances. Katy sighed. "All right. We'll see you tomorrow."

"Have fun this evening, girls." Aunt Rebecca closed the door, sealing Katy and Shelby outside.

Shelby looked at Katy. "Well ..."

Katy shrugged. "Well ..." After nearly two weeks of focusing on running the fabric shop, she wasn't sure what to do with a free afternoon. "Should we go home, or ...?"

Shelby adjusted her crutches. "Whatever you want to do is fine." She released a light laugh. "Not to be rude or anything, but what is there to do in Schellberg?"

Not as much as there is to do in Salina. Shelby would probably enjoy browsing the mall or going to a movie. But those weren't options in Katy's little Mennonite town. She gestured to the café next door. "We could get a milkshake or something."

Shelby nodded eagerly. "That sounds great. It's really hot out here."

"Then let's go."

The girls settled into a booth underneath a squeaky ceiling fan, one of three that stirred the air due to the absence of air conditioning in the café. Shelby flapped the neck of her T-shirt and grinned. "Feels good."

The café owner's daughter, Yvonne Richter, ambled to the table. Yvonne had graduated from the Schellberg school three years ahead of Katy, and even though the girls knew each other, Katy couldn't call Yvonne a friend. Unlike most of the unmarried young people, who mixed with kids older and younger, Yvonne held herself aloof from those younger than her.

"Kind of late for lunch," Yvonne said. "Dad already turned off the grill."

Katy caught the hint. "We don't want anything hot. Just milkshakes, please. Chocolate for me."

"I'd like vanilla," Shelby said.

Yvonne's tennis shoe soles squeaked as she turned and headed for the kitchen. Soon the discordant hum of a blender carried through the open doorway.

Shelby leaned forward and whispered, "She's kind of grumpy. Should we not have come in?" She glanced around the empty café. "I mean, there's nobody else here . . ."

Katy shrugged. "If they don't want business they should put out the closed sign." Remembering Yvonne's disapproving glare, she giggled. "She was probably hiding in the corner reading a romance novel and we interrupted her." Katy risked a quick look toward the kitchen, then shared,

"When we were in school, I saw Yvonne prop a romance novel behind her history book and read it when she should have been studying."

Shelby laughed. "Really? Right there in the schoolroom?"

Katy nodded.

"That's funny to think about." Shelby tipped her head, her short blonde hair whisking against her jaw. "I guess I figured kids from Schellberg are ... I don't know ... better behaved than kids in Salina. Because you're so religious. You know what I mean?"

Katy knew what Shelby meant. But kids in Schellberg were still kids, and they still did things they shouldn't sometimes. It was just harder to get by with bad behavior because parents and other members of the community kept a close watch on the town's young people. "We aren't perfect," Katy said. Sometimes she thought Dad expected her to be, though.

"No, but you're a lot closer to perfect than most people I know." Shelby traced her fingertip over the green squiggles in the table's Formica top. "Sometimes I feel downright heathen next to you in your little white cap and knee-length dress."

Katy gaped at Shelby. "Really?"

"Really."

Since Shelby was being honest, Katy admitted, "And sometimes I feel like a — a bumbling imbecile around you. You *know* so much more than I do ..."

Shelby snorted. She tucked her hair behind her ear and grinned. "Well, I guess our hanging out together proves heathens and imbeciles can still be friends, huh?"

Katy laughed, amazed at how good it felt after worrying so much about Aunt Rebecca. Rosemary was right—having Shelby there was a blessing. "I guess so."

Yvonne came from the kitchen, carrying two tall milk-shake glasses. She set them on the table—chocolate in front of Shelby and vanilla in front of Katy. She plucked paper-wrapped straws from her apron pocket and laid them between the two sweating glasses. Looking at Katy, she said, "Are you going to the Gehrings' tonight? Annika said we'll be making sundaes with homemade ice cream."

Shelby switched their glasses so they'd each have what they'd ordered. Yvonne didn't even glance at her.

Katy unwrapped her straw and pushed it through the thick milkshake. "I don't know. We haven't talked about it. We might, though. Are you going?"

Yvonne nodded. She coiled one of her cap's ribbons around her finger. "I'm taking my cousin Jonathan—he's visiting from Lancaster County."

Katy had seen a tall, blond-haired boy sitting with Yvonne's dad and brothers in worship service the Sunday before. But since Shelby had been with her, she hadn't asked anyone about him. "That's nice."

"He's staying all summer, helping at my oldest brother's farm. But he said he wished he could stay for good. He likes it here because he can drive a car. Motorized vehicles aren't allowed in his fellowship."

That's kind of a selfish reason to want to stay in Schellberg. Katy sipped her milkshake, uncertain how to respond. Why was Yvonne being so friendly? The girl had rarely spoken more than two or three words to Katy in the past.

"I think Annika's a little sweet on Jonathan." A coy smile played on Yvonne's lips. "She specifically requested he come."

Katy nearly rolled her eyes. Everyone knew Annika liked Caleb. "I'm sure she's just being polite." She stirred her milkshake with the straw, leaving a swirl in the thick chocolaty drink. "It would be pretty rude to invite you and leave your cousin out."

Yvonne shrugged. "I suppose." She continued to look directly at Katy, as if Shelby weren't there. "I suppose you're invited, since you're Annika's best friend."

"*We're* invited," Katy confirmed, hoping the other girl caught the emphasis on *we*. Would Yvonne ever acknowledge Shelby's presence?

"I'll be sure and introduce you to Jonathan," Yvonne said, moving slowly toward the kitchen. Her gaze still hadn't drifted to Shelby. "If he stays in Schellberg, he'll want to get to know everyone." She slipped through the doorway.

Katy let out a huff of annoyance. "Honestly! I'm sorry, Shelby. She was really rude to you."

Shelby shrugged with one shoulder, lifting her straw to lick drippy ice cream from the plastic tube. "No big deal. Like you said, kids are kids. She doesn't know me, so why should she talk to me?"

"Still ..." Yvonne's behavior reminded Katy of Annika when Annika had first met Shelby. Katy had invited both girls to a sleepover shortly after she started attending Salina High North, and the evening had been a disaster. Annika was still a little withdrawn around Shelby, but at least she talked to her. "The party won't be much fun for you if the others act like you aren't there. Do you want to go or just stay at my house this evening?"

Shelby slurped the last of her shake and then pushed the glass aside. "I don't want you to have to hide the whole summer just because I'm here. I think we should go." A teasing glint entered her eyes. "If they ignore me, I'll just clop 'em one with my crutch or something. That'll get their attention."

Katy giggled, imagining it. "So you want to go?"

"Why not? I love ice cream." Shelby glanced at the empty milkshake glass and giggled. "Obviously." She sobered. "And maybe if I'm around a little more, the kids will start to be more comfortable around me." She leaned back and sighed. "Sometimes, when you're different, it takes a while to settle in."

Katy nodded thoughtfully. It had taken an entire school year for her to feel comfortable at the public high school. Even then, she only felt comfortable with a small group of students. There were some who would never accept her. But she didn't really care. As long as she had her friends — Shelby, Cora, Trisha, and Bryce — she'd be happy. Thinking of Bryce, she couldn't help but smile. She looked forward to seeing him when school started again.

"All right, we'll go," Katy said.

"Good!" Shelby struggled out of the booth and slipped her crutches into position. She followed Katy to the counter. Yvonne's father came from the back and took their money. Katy gave him an extra fifty cents to give to Yvonne as a tip. Then she and Shelby headed behind Aunt Rebecca's shop where Rocky and the cart waited.

Katy helped Shelby climb in, giggling when Shelby

almost fell into the seat. Katy reached for the reins, but before she could take hold, Shelby grabbed Katy's arm.

"Katy, this party we're going to ..." Shelby tipped her head, her brow crinkling. "It's a boy-girl party, right?"

"Yes," Katy said. Most of the parties for the young people were boy-girl. Marriage matches often formed at the community parties. But she didn't bother to explain all of that to Shelby.

"Well ... maybe ... since I'm going with you, Annika wouldn't mind another person coming too?"

Katy frowned. A trickle of sweat tickled her temple, and she swished it away. "Like who?"

A sly grin crept up Shelby's cheek. "Like ... Bryce."

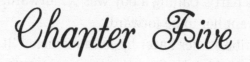

Chapter Five

"B-Bryce?" Katy flicked the reins, encouraging Rocky to pick up the pace. The sun scorched the top of her head through the mesh headcovering, and rivulets of sweat trickled between her shoulder blades. The sooner they reached the farm and got out of the heat, the better.

"Sure, Bryce." Shelby leaned into the corner of the seat and squinted at Katy. "I've got his phone number, and didn't he tell you on the last day of school he'd like to see you over the summer?"

Katy nodded, remembering their last conversation. He'd been so sweet, telling her to have a good summer but give him a call if she wanted company—he'd drive out to see her. She'd giggled in pleased embarrassment when he'd given her a little square of paper with his telephone number scrawled on it in green ink. Green ink ... like the color of his eyes. She sighed. "It would be fun to see Bryce."

"Well, then, would Annika mind if he came to her party? Will there be enough food for one more?"

"Her mom always makes plenty—I doubt food's a problem." But Katy wasn't sure she should call and invite Bryce to Annika's party. Calling a boy was … forward. And Dad wouldn't want her to be forward.

Shelby nibbled her lower lip for a moment. "If he came too, then I wouldn't be the only, you know, outsider."

Katy sent Shelby a surprised look. "Do you really feel that out of place?" Then she mentally kicked herself for asking. Of course Shelby felt out of place! With every girl in Schellberg wearing dresses and white caps with trailing ribbons and Shelby dressed in capri pants and T-shirts, Shelby stuck out like Katy did in the public high school. Katy knew how it felt to be the person who was different. Even though Shelby was willing to go to the party, she'd still be apprehensive. It made sense.

Shelby said, "It's a little weird." She tucked her hair behind her ear. "I mean, I'm glad to be here and all, even though I'd really wanted to go on that mission trip. And now that your aunt's sick, it's great that I can help out — makes me feel not so bad about having to stay behind while my family's serving in Africa." She blew out a little breath that ruffled her bangs. "Really, Katy, how'd you keep showing up at school day after day with the way the kids treated you the first few weeks? I'd have probably run home to hide under the bed if it had been me getting all those stares and stupid comments."

Katy offered a shrug, tugging the reins to slow Rocky on the corner. Dust billowed, tickling her nose. A car would sure be a more comfortable means of transport. "I did it because I wanted to go to high school. It was my only option."

"You know, there are other options for school," Shelby said. "You could take online classes through the Saline

County Education Cooperative and then take your GED test."

Katy frowned. "What?"

"Online courses—you know, working on a computer instead of going to class." Shelby slapped her forehead. "Oh, duh. You don't have a computer. Never mind." She shook her head, making her hair flop. "Forget I said anything. Back to the party ... I have my cell phone." Grinning, she patted her pocket. "Should I call Bryce?"

Katy's mouth felt dry. She wished she had another milkshake to sip. "Let's check with Annika's mother first, okay?" They had to drive past the Gehrings' place to get to Katy's farm, so it wasn't out of the way. And if Mrs. Gehring said no, it would settle things. *Do I want her to say yes or no about inviting Bryce?* Katy wasn't sure of the answer.

✢

Mrs. Gehring approved inviting Bryce, and Annika said her party would start at eight o'clock. Since the milking was finished by six thirty, Caleb would have had plenty of time to go home, eat supper, clean up, and change clothes. But for reasons Katy couldn't understand, Dad had told him to bring his clean clothes and change at their house after supper. So Caleb was sitting in the front room with Shelby, Katy, and Katy's parents when Bryce's car pulled into the driveway at a quarter 'til eight.

Katy heard the crunch of tires on gravel and jumped up. Unconsciously, she smoothed the skirt of her lavender floral dress then adjusted the ties of her cap to hang neatly across her shoulders. She caught Caleb's frown, realized she was preening, and clasped her hands together. She bobbed her chin toward the back of the house.

"Bryce is here." Why did she sound like her vocal cords had been tied in a knot? She cleared her throat and said, "Dad, should I ...? Or will you ...?" She'd never had a boy—other than Caleb—come to her house before. How did a girl greet a male visitor?

Rosemary and Dad exchanged a quick grin. Rosemary said, "Why don't you welcome our guest, Samuel?"

Dad strode past Katy and went to the back door. A squeak of hinges let Katy know Dad held the door open, waiting for Bryce to approach. She stood rooted in the middle of the front room, leaning sideways slightly to peer through the wide dining room doorway. At that angle, she could barely see the narrow opening to the mudroom off the kitchen. She couldn't see Dad or Bryce, but she heard Dad say, "Hello," and then Bryce's answer, "Good evening, Mr. and Mrs. Lambright."

At the sound of his voice, her heart bounced around in her chest like a Ping-Pong ball. She scurried to the couch and sat next to Shelby so Bryce wouldn't find her standing in the center of the area rug like a misplaced statue. She felt Caleb's glare on her, but she didn't look at him. Instead, she watched the doorway, and her breath sped into little gasps when Bryce followed Dad into the front room.

Bryce's gaze met Katy's, and he smiled. "Hi, Katy."

Katy jolted to her feet, her face breaking into an answering smile. "Hi, Bryce."

He glanced at Shelby and lifted his hand in a wave. Then he turned toward Caleb. For a moment, he seemed to freeze, then he walked over and held out his hand. "Hi. I'm Bryce."

Caleb stared at Bryce's hand for a few seconds before giving it a brief shake. But he didn't stand up, which made it awkward. "I'm Caleb Penner. I work for Mr. Lambright." Caleb's voice came out defensive, as if Bryce had accused him of something improper.

Bryce just nodded. "Nice to meet you."

Looking at Bryce and Caleb side by side, Katy was struck anew by how they resembled each other, with their short-cropped, reddish-cast hair, green-blue eyes, and spattering of freckles. But Bryce was more handsome than Caleb. At least in Katy's opinion.

Rosemary crossed to Katy and put her arm around her shoulders. "Well, you young folks should probably head over to the Gehrings' now. I imagine they'll have a crowd, and the ice cream will go fast. I'd hate to see you miss out on such a treat."

Katy had counted eight ice cream freezers on Annika's front porch, which seemed like a lot. But considering the appetites of some of the young men, Rosemary might be right. She turned to Shelby. "Are you ready?"

"Yep." Shelby had donned a simple midcalf-length flowered skirt with her T-shirt so she wouldn't be the only girl wearing pants. She'd also tied her hair into a messy little ponytail at the base of her skull. Wispy strands too short for the tail hung along her cheeks with a few other strands tucked behind her ears. She looked so cute and feminine, Katy almost felt jealous. Why would Bryce want to spend time with Katy when someone like Shelby was available?

With a slight frown on his face, Bryce watched Shelby stump across the floor with her crutches. "I brought my dad's car. It's a two-door, so Shelby'll need to sit in the front seat. It'll be easier for her to get in and out." He sent an apologetic look in Katy's direction. "Do you mind riding in the back seat?" His gaze skittered to Caleb and then to Katy again. "There's room for Caleb too."

"I have my own car," Caleb blurted. He pushed his hands into the pockets of his trousers. "And mine's got *four* doors, so the girls can ride with me."

Katy's ears heated. Did Caleb think he was in competition with Bryce? *As if!* All the warm feelings she'd had for him when he offered to help Aunt Rebecca and Uncle Albert fled.

Dad coughed into his hand, the way he did when he was trying to hide a laugh. He said, "I suppose the girls could just take the two-wheeled cart and follow you boys."

Both Katy and Shelby said, "No thank you!"

Dad laughed out loud.

Rosemary intervened. "I'm sure Bryce will want to head straight home after the party, but Caleb has to drive past our place to get to his house. Maybe you girls could ride with Bryce to the party and with Caleb on the way home." Her diplomatic suggestion made sense to Katy, but Caleb mumbled something under his breath.

"What was that, Caleb?" Rosemary asked.

He shrugged, scowling. "Nothing. I'll meet you at Annika's." He charged out the door. His car zoomed out of the yard just as Katy and the others stepped outside.

Dad and Rosemary followed Bryce and the girls to Bryce's car. Katy tried not to gawk. Bold cherry-red, sporty-looking, with two wide white stripes running from the hood, over the top, and across the back hatch, the car had a sleek appearance that caught the eye. No one in Schellberg drove a car anything like it.

Dad released a low whistle. "You said this is your dad's car?"

Bryce patted the striped hood. "Yes, sir. He bought it when he graduated from high school in 1979. It's a Chevy Nova—the last model manufactured."

Dad whistled again. "Nice wheels."

Katy nearly swallowed her tongue. She'd never heard Dad use a phrase like that before!

Bryce grinned. "My dad thinks so too. I have to promise to be very careful whenever I drive it."

Dad nodded. "I can see why." He circled the car with his hands in his pockets, examining it.

Bryce opened the passenger door and folded the front seat forward. He offered a lop-sided smile to Katy. "It's hard to get in, but the back seat's pretty comfortable once you're settled."

Katy flashed a quick answering grin, mindful that Dad and Rosemary were watching. "I'll be fine." She clambered into the back, wishing Bryce's car had one long seat in the front instead of two individual seats separated by some sort of console. Then she could have slid into the middle and sat between Bryce and Shelby. The thought of being snuggled up close to Bryce made her heart pound.

Bryce snapped the seat into place and held Shelby's crutches while she slid in. Then he angled the crutches in next to Shelby, closed the door, and trotted to the driver's side.

Dad leaned forward to peek inside the car as Bryce started the engine. "You kids have fun. Behave."

"We will," Katy and Shelby choroused.

Bryce pulled forward slowly. He didn't spin his tires. At the end of the driveway, he spoke over the engine's purr. "Which way?"

"West," Katy answered, scooting forward and propping her arms on the back of Shelby's seat. "It's just a mile to the Gehrings' farm. You can follow Caleb's trail." Dust still hung in little clouds where Caleb had driven a few minutes earlier.

Bryce sent a smile over his shoulder. "Will do." He pushed the gas pedal, and the car turned onto the road.

Katy looked out the back window. Dad and Rosemary stood in the yard, their arms looped around one another's waists. They looked so peaceful together — so right. Katy waved and then faced forward, her gaze finding Bryce's profile and lingering. A little pang stabbed her heart. Dad and Rosemary fit because they were both Mennonite. They believed the same way — lived the same simple way. As much as she liked Bryce, they'd never fit together the way Dad and Rosemary did. She was Mennonite; Bryce was not. It was foolish to spend time with him this way.

But instead of asking him to take her back home, she pointed at Annika's turnoff. "Right here."

"Gotcha," Bryce said cheerfully. He drove up the driveway. Several guys, including Caleb, milled in the yard. They watched Bryce's car approach, nudging each other or pointing. Katy imagined the guys asking who was coming and Caleb answering in a derisive tone, "Oh, one of Katy's *Salina* friends."

Nervousness made her skin go clammy. Her heart thudded hard, making her ears ring. Should she have brought Bryce? It might give people — Bryce included — the wrong idea. *This could be an interesting evening ...*

Chapter Six

Groups parted, creating a pathway that led to the Gehrings' front porch. Bryce walked slowly, allowing Shelby to keep up, but Katy wished they could run and get past the others quickly. Conversations fell away and curious gazes followed them.

Even though no one except Caleb seemed outright suspicious of the newcomers, Katy still experienced a rush of frustration. Couldn't someone — *anyone* — say hello? Instead they gawked, silent and uncertain. Katy tried to act natural, sauntering between Bryce and Shelby while looking across the yard. Annika's mother had attempted to give the area a festive appearance. Picnic tables wearing bright, checked cloths dotted the sparse grass that served as the Gehrings' front yard. The Gehrings didn't have a lush yard — they had too many little boys who liked to play on the grass to keep it nice. But the bright splashes of color from the tablecloths made the brown patches of worn-out grass look cheerful.

If only the kids acted more cheerful instead of standoff-ish. Katy stifled a sigh.

Annika's mother smiled brightly when they reached the edge of the porch. To Katy's relief, she didn't seem apprehensive at all about having Bryce and Shelby there, even smiling broadly at Shelby as they approached. "Annika just ran in to start whipping the cream. She wanted it to be fresh," Mrs. Gehring said. She wiped her hand on her apron and held it out to Bryce. "I'm Mrs. Gehring. You must be Katy's friend Bryce."

Bryce shook Mrs. Gehring's hand. "Yes, ma'am. Thank you for letting me come tonight." His gaze whisked across the row of ice cream freezers and the table cluttered with various sundae toppings. "Wow, this looks great."

Mrs. Gehring laughed. "I'm sure it won't last long, though." She leaned forward slightly and said in a confidential manner, "I've got two more freezers in the kitchen as backup, just in case. But don't tell the older boys—if they think this is it, they might not be so greedy right from the start."

Katy had seen some of the older boys dive into the plates of sandwiches and cookies at other parties without regard for anyone else, but she didn't want to sound like a talebearer, so she kept the thought to herself. "Should I give Annika a hand?" she asked.

Mrs. Gehring shook her head. "You stay out here and mingle, Katy. You've been working extra hard at Rebecca's—you've earned a little time off." She headed into the house, letting the screen door slam behind her.

The kids had begun chatting again, their combined voices filling the yard. Katy turned to Shelby and Bryce. "Do you want to sit down, or—"

A group of three older boys, with Caleb leading the pack, strode up to Katy and her friends. Caleb said, "Hey. Todd, Anton, and Justin want to look at your car."

Katy bristled. Couldn't Caleb introduce Bryce to the other boys before making a demand? That boy had no manners whatsoever. She adopted a sweet tone and said, "Bryce, you've already met Caleb. This is Todd Schenk, Anton Friesen, and Justin Keiler." She pointed to each boy by turn, and they offered shy nods of hello, which Bryce returned.

Caleb scowled. "So can we look at your car or not?"

Bryce shoved his hands into the pockets of his jeans. "Sure, it's fine. It's not mine, though. It's my dad's."

Katy thought it was very honest of Bryce to admit the car didn't belong to him.

A smirk twisted Caleb's lips. "You don't have your own car?" He nudged Todd, who stood the closest to him. "We all have our own cars already."

Katy wanted to kick Caleb in the shins, but Bryce shrugged, seemingly unaffected by Caleb's gibe. "Haven't needed my own yet since Dad lets me borrow his. I'm saving up for one, though — I know I'll need one when I go to college." He tipped his head and squinted. "So ... you wanna look at the Nova?"

"Sure," Justin and Anton said at the same time and Todd nodded.

Bryce touched Katy's arm. "I'll be back in a little bit."

Katy watched Bryce amble off with Justin, Todd, and Anton, her heart fluttering. Looking at the four boys together — each wearing tucked-in shirts with jeans or trousers—Bryce appeared to be another Mennonite boy attending a youth gathering. And he seemed completely at ease in this new surrounding. Her heart fluttered harder.

Caleb tapped her arm, bringing her attention to him. "Was that supposed to be some kind of put-down— mentioning college?"

Katy blinked twice, confused. What was Caleb talking about? Then she remembered Bryce's comment about needing a car for college and rolled her eyes. Bryce wasn't vindictive. He wouldn't deliberately insult anyone even if they deserved it, which—in Katy's opinion—Caleb did. Bryce's kindness was one of the things she liked best about him.

"Like he's supposed to know our fellowship doesn't attend college," Katy said, allowing sarcasm to color her tone. "You were the one being snide, Caleb, bragging about how you own a car already. What's your problem?"

Caleb's scowl deepened. "Don't use your fancy words on me, Katydid." He spat the nickname he'd used to irritate her when they were younger. "I don't have a problem, but you must, if the boys around here aren't good enough for you. You have to date a worldly boy in a worldly car to show off."

Katy stared at Caleb, her ears so hot she wondered if smoke rose from them. She glanced toward the others, and relief nearly buckled her knees when she realized no one was paying any attention to Caleb and her. Caleb's behavior was embarrassing, but at least they didn't have an audience. Except for Shelby, who tactfully looked off to the side and pretended not to listen.

Keeping her voice low but emphatic, Katy said, "Listen, Caleb, Bryce is just my friend, and—"

Caleb threw his hand in the air. "I don't want to hear your excuses." He shot a quick look at Shelby, and for a moment he looked embarrassed. Then his face hardened. "You need to watch yourself, Katy. Decide who your friends are going to be — kids from the fellowship or kids from Salina. Remember you're not supposed to be a part of the world." He whirled and stomped off before Katy could reply.

Hurt and fury battled for first place in Katy's feelings. Her chin quivered.

Shelby leaned close and bumped shoulders with her. "Hey ... are you okay? Do you want to leave?"

Katy folded her arms over her chest and set her jaw. She blinked rapidly. "No, I don't want to leave. That's what *he* wants me to do — to run home in shame." She glared at Shelby. "Well, I'm not ashamed of my friendship with you or ... or with Bryce! You're both good friends to me. You're Christians too, even if you aren't Mennonite. It's Caleb" — she swung her hand in the direction Caleb had disappeared — "who has the problem."

Shelby cleared her throat, her gaze shifting to something behind Katy. Katy whirled around and found herself face-to-face with the tall, slender, blond-haired boy she'd seen in church service last Sunday. He looked directly into her face, and when he smiled, his dark-blue eyes lit up.

"Hi."

Katy gulped. "Hi."

Yvonne Richter stepped up beside the boy. She curled her hands around his arm. "Katy, this is my cousin, Jonathan — Jonathan Richter. Jonathan, this is Kathleen Lambright. Everybody calls her Katy."

Jonathan nodded at Katy. "It's nice to meet you, Katy."
Then he looked at Shelby. "And this is ...?"

Yvonne dipped her head for a moment. "This is Katy's
friend from Salina. I don't remember her name."

Katy said, "Shelby Nuss."

"Hi, Shelby," Jonathan said, his voice as warm and
friendly in greeting Shelby as he'd been greeting Katy.

"Hi," Shelby said. She shifted a bit, adjusting her
crutches. "I hate to be a party pooper, but I'm really tired
of standing here. Do you mind if I ...?" She started inching toward a picnic table.

Jonathan darted forward and pulled out a folding chair
for her. "There you go. I bet it's hard, leaning on those
crutches all the time. How much longer will you have to
use them?"

Shelby sank onto the seat and set her crutches aside.
"'Til the end of August or so. Then I'll get a walking
boot."

Katy stood, staring in disbelief as Jonathan and Shelby
visited like old friends. Then he turned around and caught
Katy's eye. "Did you want to sit down too?" He grabbed a
second chair.

Wow ... he's so polite! Katy scurried to the chair. "Yes.
Yes, I do. Thanks." She sat next to Shelby, her eyes pinned
to Jonathan's face. She hadn't noticed in church how nice-
looking he was. Realizing what she was thinking, she felt
her ears heat up.

Yvonne captured Jonathan's arm again. "Come on. I
want to go talk to Sheila and Bonnie."

"Sure, Yvonne." Jonathan bobbed his head first at
Shelby then at Katy. "It was very nice to meet you, Shelby

and Katy. Maybe we'll talk more ... later." Yvonne tugged his arm, and he trotted off with her.

Katy watched after them. Even though she'd only just met Jonathan, she wished he'd stayed a little longer. He'd mostly talked to Shelby. She wanted him to talk to her too.

A giggle rang, and she turned to find Shelby grinning at her. The heat from her ears flooded into her cheeks. "What?"

Shelby bobbed her chin toward Jonathan then smiled at Katy again. "Is Bryce getting a little competition from the visiting Mennonite from Lancaster County?"

"Competition ..." Katy snorted, but she knew it wasn't very convincing. "It's not like Bryce is my boyfriend." Her gaze searched the crowd for Bryce. She found him beside his dad's car, gesturing with one hand while he talked with Justin, Anton, and Todd. Again, she noticed how well Bryce fit in with the Mennonite boys, looks-wise. *But he isn't Mennonite*, she reminded herself.

Unconsciously, her attention shifted and she spotted Jonathan with Yvonne and her friends. While she watched, he turned his head and caught her looking. He smiled. She jerked her face toward Shelby, her heart thudding wildly. Jonathan was nice, like Bryce. And good-looking, like Bryce. But unlike Bryce, he was Mennonite. Dad would surely approve if—

She bounced up, unwilling to let her thoughts carry her any further. "Will you be okay for a few minutes, Shelby? I'd like to go hurry Annika up. I'm ready for some ice cream." She dashed for the house as if Dad's bull chased her.

✤

Katy waited until Shelby fell asleep before creeping out from between the sheets and tiptoeing to her desk. She removed her journal from the drawer, grimacing when the wood released a high-pitched whine of complaint. But Shelby didn't stir. Journal and pencil in hand, Katy crossed the staircase landing and entered the room that used to be her sewing room but now served as a guest room for Rosemary's children when they visited. She closed the door before pulling the string for the overhead light—she didn't want to disturb anyone. Then she perched on the edge of the bed and opened her journal.

Rarely had she gone more than a week without recording her thoughts in the spiral-bound notebook, but between Shelby's visit and spending so many hours at Aunt Rebecca's shop, her journal had been neglected. Tonight, however, she had to write. The evening's events—having three boys vie for her attention, being with her Salina friends and her Schellberg friends in the same place, and experiencing a whirlwind of emotions—left her feeling restless and in need of answers. She always found release in writing.

She began to scribble, recording bits and pieces of the evening. Her frustration with Caleb's jealous reaction to Bryce's presence, her relief at Bryce's easy way of talking with the Schellberg kids, and her heart-fluttering pleasure at Jonathan's consideration poured onto the page.

Jonathan even offered to hold my sundae so I could dish up Shelby's ice cream, letting his melt while he waited on me, she wrote, the lines of print wavering a bit as her hand trembled. He'd been so sweetly attentive to both Katy and Shelby. Her heart fluttered again, just thinking about the way Jonathan acted. He was so nice.

Midway through the party, Annika had whispered in Katy's ear, "I think Jonathan likes you." Katy hadn't needed Annika to suggest it—she'd already suspected as much. And, she admitted, she liked Jonathan too. But how could she like Jonathan when she already liked Bryce? Was it fair? And which boy should she like—Bryce, who wasn't Mennonite but who'd been her friend for several months; or Jonathan, a Mennonite boy who'd only just arrived in Schellberg and would be leaving at the end of the summer?

A poem began to form in her head, and she transferred it to the page.

> *Two worlds, two ways of living a life—*
> *Each offering portions of joy and strife.*
> *But in which world do I belong?*
> *Where will my heart sing its perfect song?*
> *In either I can keep my faith,*
> *But only in one will I find the grace*
> *And acceptance of those I hold most dear . . .*
>
> *Two hearts, two boys who tug at me—*
> *Who bid me to discover what might be.*
> *But with which one do I belong?*
> *Can caring for either of them be wrong?*
> *They each possess a heart of faith,*
> *But only one can take his place*
> *In my life; one would pull me away from here . . .*

She slapped the journal closed and hugged the book to her chest. What was she doing, sitting here late at night worrying about boys? She'd always disdained Annika's infatuation with boys. Last year, when Shelby had a boyfriend, Katy resented the silly way her friend acted around Jayden. Katy didn't want to get caught up in all the ridiculous giggling and flirting and changing that seemed to accompany having a boyfriend. Yet at the same time, she thrilled at the idea of having a boy like her. Really, really like her.

She lowered the notebook to her lap and opened it again, gazing down at the line *But only one can take his place* ... Katy closed her eyes and whispered into the empty room, "God, right now my place is helping Aunt Rebecca. I need to focus on her, not on myself and Bryce or Jonathan. So would You please take these silly ideas out of my head?"

But even after Katy slipped back into bed, images of the two boys continued to play in her mind's eye.

Chapter Seven

On Saturday, after closing the fabric shop, Shelby asked Katy to drive Caleb's horse cart to the pasture so she could get a look at Shadow's foal, Saydee. Although Katy had checked on the horses each day, ascertaining they had a good supply of water in the tank and feeding them a portion of oats, Shelby had stayed at the house with Rosemary instead of accompanying Katy.

"The worst part of having these crutches," Shelby groused when Katy drew the cart to a stop along the fence line, "is not being able to walk out, pet the horses, or maybe ride Shadow."

Katy said, "You might not be able to walk out with them or take a ride, but I can get them to come to you so you can pet them." She climbed down and moved to the barbed wire fence that enclosed the pasture. Placing two fingers in her mouth, she released a shrill whistle. Shadow immediately galloped over, and Saydee followed on long, spindly legs.

Shelby squealed in delight. She clambered off the cart and limped to the fence. "Oh, Katy, the little one is so sweet! Will she let me pet her?"

Katy grimaced. "I'm not sure."

Saydee had spent most of her first weeks of life only with her mother. Katy hoped not socializing the colt wouldn't create problems later on. If Saydee were to be a good cart-pulling horse someday, she needed to be at ease with human contact. As soon as things settled down, Katy needed to spend extra time with the colt.

"But," she added, "Shadow will let you pet her. She loves to have her chin scratched."

Shelby reached for the foal—a miniature version of her mother—first, but as Katy feared, Saydee shied away. With a sigh, Shelby curved her hand under Shadow's jaw. While she scratched Shadow, she gazed longingly at the colt. "I love her black mane and tail against the tawny brown of her coat. And that white diamond on her forehead makes her look so sweet." She sighed again. "Such a little beauty ..."

Katy agreed. Saydee had all the markings of becoming a beautiful horse. But she'd be useless if she was afraid of people. "I need to get out here more. The first year of socializing an animal is the most important. If Saydee spends all her time with Shadow, she might never learn to bond with humans."

"So come out more often," Shelby said. "I don't mind."

Katy didn't answer. Shelby couldn't understand that Saydee needed more than a brief visit each day with someone reaching over the fence to try to stroke her nose or neck. Katy needed to get into the pasture with Saydee— to walk beside her, talk to her, earn her trust. Watching the colt hide behind its mother, peering out with wide, apprehensive brown eyes and snorting now and then in nervousness, made Katy realize how much she'd ne-glected the animal. But how could she give Saydee what she needed when she was working all day, every day, in Schellberg at the fabric shop and spending her evenings with Shelby?

If Shelby didn't have to rely on the crutches, then both girls could socialize the colt. *But if Shelby didn't have the crutches, she wouldn't even be here,* Katy reminded herself. She wouldn't wish away her time with her friend — she enjoyed Shelby's company, and she was great help at the shop. She only wished she could have Shelby's companion-ship *and* time with Saydee. She scolded herself: *And since when have you gotten so selfish, Kathleen Lambright?*

Stepping away from the fence, Katy said, "I guess we'd better head to the house. Rosemary will wonder what's keeping us. She knows the shop closed at noon."

Shelby reluctantly backed up a step, stumbling a bit as she planted the tip of her crutch in the weed-strewn ditch. "If you had a phone at the house, I could call and tell her where we are."

There was no point in complaining about the lack of telephones. The deacons had postponed making a deci-sion, wanting to check with other fellowships and explore all the possible social and spiritual ramifications before changing the fellowship dictate concerning the use of phones. So no telephone in Katy's house. And no cell phone in Katy's pocket.

Katy helped Shelby into the cart then started to climb in on the opposite side. Before she could pull herself onto the seat, though, the honk of a car's horn intruded. She looked down the road to see a dark green pickup truck approaching—Dan Richter's truck. The sun glinted on the windshield, hiding the driver from view until it pulled alongside the cart. Then Katy's heart jolted.

Jonathan!

He left the engine idling when he got out, and the steady rumble matched the thrumming beat of Katy's heart.

"Hi." He pointed to the horses in the enclosure. "Are they yours?"

Katy nodded. Her tongue felt stuck to the roof of her mouth. She hadn't felt so wordless in a boy's presence since her early days of infatuation with Bryce. It left her unsettled.

"I've watched them when I've driven by before," he said. He slipped his hands into his pockets and looked toward the horses. A soft smile curved his lips. "The colt has great lines."

Katy turned and watched Saydee dip her nose toward a cluster of grass then jolt upright, shake her mane, and dance in a circle. She couldn't stop a giggle from rising in her throat. The foal reminded her of a playful, overgrown puppy. "Thanks. I think she's pretty special."

"I tried to coax her into letting me pet her," Jonathan went on.

Katy looked at him, surprised. "You did?"

He shrugged, and his grin turned sheepish. "Yeah. My dad and uncle raise horses in Lancaster County. I miss being around them. So when I spotted the mare and foal, I couldn't resist trying to make friends." He rocked on his heels. "You don't mind, do you?"

Wheels began spinning in the back of Katy's mind.

"No. No, not at all. They need more attention than I've been able to give them lately. Anytime you'd like to come out and talk to them, pet them, whatever ... you're more than welcome."

"Thanks. I appreciate that."

"Thank *you.*"

For several seconds they stood, silent, staring into each other's faces. Then Shelby cleared her throat, and Katy jumped.

"Oh! I need to be getting home now, but ..." She backed toward the cart, waving her hand in the direction of the pasture. "Feel free to visit Shadow and Saydee anytime."

He trotted after her. "Katy, wait!"

She paused at the edge of the cart, her hand on the seat's armrest.

Jonathan's grin spread, his eyes twinkling. "Which one is which?"

Heat filled Katy's ears. "Shadow's the mom, Saydee's the baby."

"Great names."

The heat in her ears increased. She knew they were blazing red, and she wanted to hide. She scrambled into the cart's seat and plucked up the reins. "I have to go now, Jonathan. Bye!"

Katy brought down the reins on Rocky's back, and he snorted as he jolted forward. The cart rolled from the ditch and onto the road. She let Rocky trot briskly for a half mile, carrying them well away from Jonathan, before she pulled back on the reins and said, "Whoa there, Rocky, slow down."

Shelby let out a big breath. "Whew ... I thought you

were going to run him all the way home." She swiped
her hand across her brow, removing sweat and dust.
"What's your rush? Did Jonathan make a pass at you or
something?"

Katy gave her friend a horrified look. "Of course not!"

"Then why the hurry to get away from him?"

Katy didn't know why she'd felt the need to escape. But
talking to Jonathan gave her a funny feeling in the pit of
her stomach—a feeling she didn't know how to cope with.
"I—I just knew we needed to get home. So Rosemary
wouldn't worry."

"Mm-hm." Shelby didn't ask for a further explanation.

When they reached the farm, Katy pulled Rocky to
the back door of the house and helped Shelby down. "I'm
going to put Rocky in the corral beside the barn and give
him some hay and water. I'll be in soon—can you tell
Rosemary?"

"Sure." Shelby hitched herself onto the stoop and entered the house.

Katy grabbed Rocky's bridle and led him to the barn. As
she began to release the riggings from his head, Dad came
out of the room where the milk tank was stored.

"Oh, Katy-girl, I'm glad you're home. I need to talk to
you."

Katy held tight to Rocky's bridle and faced her dad. Dad
jammed his hands into the pockets of his grubby coveralls.
The gesture reminded her of Bryce—he often stood with
his hands in his pockets, his feet widespread. With a start,
she realized Jonathan had stood the same way when talking to her at the fence. She shook her head, sending the
images away. "About what?"

"Monday." He pulled one hand free to stroke Rocky's glistening neck. "Rebecca's surgery is scheduled for eight in the morning, so she needs to be at the hospital by six. Gramma and Grampa would like to be with her, as does Albert, of course. Since the fabric shop's never open on Mondays and you won't be working, they wondered if you and Shelby would mind staying in town Sunday night with Albert and Rebecca. That way you can help the twins with the younger kids until Albert gets home later in the afternoon."

Katy didn't even have to think about it. "Sure, we can do that." She tipped her head. "Are you and Rosemary going to the hospital too?"

"Rosemary might—she hasn't decided yet, but I'll stay here. Gotta milk, you know."

For as long as Katy could remember, the cows had always come first. She wondered if Dad felt guilty, taking care of cows when his only brother's wife was undergoing surgery. But she wouldn't ask. "Whatever we can do, Dad, we're willing."

Dad gave Katy a rare hug. He smelled of the barn, but she didn't mind. She hugged him in return, hard, then stepped away. She started to guide Rocky out of the barn, but Dad called her back again.

"What are you and Shelby doing this afternoon?"

Katy wanted to return to the pasture and spend a little time with Saydee, but it depended on Shelby's ankle. "I'm not sure yet. Why?"

"Rosemary might need your help." Dad scratched his chin. His brow furrowed into lines of worry. "She and several of the ladies are putting together a luncheon for tomorrow after service for the entire fellowship — for Aunt Rebecca. Afterward, they'll take a love offering to help with the hospital expenses."

Katy nodded. Often the fellowship came together in support of a member who needed financial assistance, and she'd hoped someone would organize something for Aunt Rebecca. She could set aside visiting Saydee for the sake of her aunt. "Sure, we'll help."

Dad's approving smile warmed Katy. "I figured you would. She was hesitant to ask you, since you've taken on so much responsibility at the fabric shop."

Even though Katy was working more at the fabric shop, her responsibilities at home were less than they'd been before Dad married Rosemary. Rosemary did half of the household chores and most of the cooking. In fact, Katy had fewer responsibilities in the house than she'd had since she turned twelve years old.

Dad added, "She doesn't want to burden you."

Katy wanted to appreciate Rosemary's concern, but for some reason the statement bothered her. Probably because it insinuated Dad and Rosemary had been talking *about* her instead of *to* her. She'd never liked that.

"Helping my family isn't a burden, Dad," Katy said firmly, "and I'll go tell Rosemary so right now." She saw to Rocky's needs then hurried to the house. When she entered the kitchen, the wonderful aroma of fruit pies greeted her nose. Shelby sat at the table with a large wedge of blueberry pie topped with whipped cream in front of her.

"Mrs. Lambright's been baking," Shelby said.

Katy nodded in acknowledgment then crossed to the sink to wash her hands. Rosemary stood close by, slicing apples into a bowl. "Rosemary, if you ever need my help with anything, will you please just ask me? You don't have to ask Dad first." She made sure to maintain a respectful tone as she said, "If I don't have time for something or I'd rather not do it, I'll let you know, but don't be afraid to ask me, all right?"

Rosemary sent her a surprised look that quickly changed into a smile. "Why, of course, Katy." She laughed softly, shaking her head. The black ribbons of her cap swayed beneath her chin. "I'm still feeling my way with you. I don't want to make mistakes."

Katy softened. This developing relationship between stepmother and stepdaughter was probably awkward for Rosemary too. She tipped her lips into a teasing grin. "I won't keep track of your mistakes if you won't keep track of mine."

Rosemary's laughter increased. "Deal."

Katy blew out a breath. She wiped her hands on a towel and looked around the kitchen. "Okay. So what do you need me to do to help with tomorrow's luncheon?"

Rosemary pointed with her chin. "See that basket of cherries?" A bushel basket filled with bright red cherries sat beside the basement door. "Those have been washed, but they need to be pitted so I can bake them in a cobbler."

Katy slapped her hand to her cheek. "There are so many of them!" She picked up the basket and set it on the table. Lifting one cherry to her mouth, she said, "Where'd you get them?"

"The Richters' nephew — the one staying with their oldest boy this summer ... I think his name is Jonathan — "

Katy dropped the cherry.

" — picked them from the tree in their yard and brought them out this morning." Rosemary shook her head, chuckling. "He must have risen at the break of dawn to be able to bring them out as early as he did. But ..." She shrugged. "If he was willing to pick them, I'm willing to turn them into cobblers. That is, if you girls are willing to pit them."

Shelby's grin turned impish. She whispered, "Just think, Katy ... the very pieces of fruit you're holding in your two little hands were first held by Jonathan Richter."

Katy's ears burned hot. She hissed, "Shelby ... you hush up!"

Chapter Eight

Katy stood behind the dessert table and dished servings of pie, cake, brownies, and cobblers. She hid a yawn behind her hand—she and Rosemary had stayed up until almost midnight baking pies and cobblers. Although she was tired and her feet hurt, her heart thrilled at the wonderful turnout for Aunt Rebecca's luncheon.

During worship service that morning, the deacons held a special prayer time for Aunt Rebecca, filling Katy's heart with hope that her aunt would be just fine. After the service, Aunt Rebecca stood at the basement doorway and received hugs and words of encouragement as people filed downstairs to eat. Katy couldn't help but marvel at the change she witnessed in her aunt. Aunt Rebecca had never been one to openly embrace people, but today she wrapped her arms around men and women, young and old, and clung. Cancer had tried to take something away from her, but in a very real sense it seemed to have given her something precious too.

The basement meeting room rang with conversation and laughter—a merry gathering in spite of its purpose.

Every fellowship member stayed for lunch, with many of the women bustling back and forth from the kitchen with fresh casserole dishes, baskets of bread, and bowls of salads of every variety. Katy had never seen so much food. The meal rivaled the dinners that took place after Christmas and Thanksgiving services. But best of all, the love offering basket sitting on a small table in the corner of the room overflowed with bills. The money would help Aunt Rebecca's family so much with the hospital expenses.

Grampa Ben approached the dessert table and perused the remaining items, his lips puckered in thought. "Hmm," he said with a wink, "guess I'll have me some of the blackberry cobbler. It's almost gone, which tells me it's good stuff."

Katy laughed at his reasoning as she scooped a sizable serving on Grampa's plate. "Do you want whipped cream too?"

"Does a chicken have feathers?"

Katy laughed again and plopped a huge dollop of whipped cream on top of the cobbler. "There you go, Grampa."

"Thank you, Katy-girl."

She watched Grampa amble back to the table where Gramma Ruthie, Dad, Uncle Albert, and Aunt Rebecca sat. As he plunked into his chair, he stuck his finger into the whipped cream and carried it to his mouth. Katy shook her head, still smiling. She loved Grampa Ben's silliness. Uncle Albert was often silly too, unlike Dad, who was much more serious. Lately, however, Uncle Albert had lost his sparkle — worry about Aunt Rebecca stole his silly side. So it gave Katy a lift to see Grampa being lighthearted instead of melancholy.

Rosemary bustled out of the kitchen. She scooped the remaining two pieces of a peach pie into a half-empty apple pie tin and picked up the empty pan. "I think there's another peach pie in the kitchen — I'll go see." Then she peeked into the bowl holding a tiny fluff of whipped cream along the sides and bottom. "Oh, my, you're getting low. I better whip up another batch of cream."

Katy said, "Will it be eaten? It's slowing down now. I think people have just about had as much as they want to eat."

Rosemary glanced across the crowded room. Tables filled the area, and nearly every seat was filled. Voices echoed from the walls and ceiling of the basement. "But they don't seem to be in any hurry to leave, do they? If they stay and visit, they might want a second dessert, so ..." She snatched up the whipped cream bowl and hurried back to the small kitchen in the corner of the basement.

Katy rearranged the pans on the table to hide the spot where the peach pie tin had sat. When she moved the cobbler pan, she accidentally stuck her thumb into a blob of gooey cherry filling. Without thinking she carried her thumb to her mouth to lick it clean. Just as she put her thumb into her mouth, Jonathan Richter stepped up to the table.

"Hey, save some for me."

Katy whipped her hand away from her face and hid it behind her back. Her ears flamed, and she wished she could pull the tablecloth over her head. "H-hi, Jonathan. Did you want some cherry cobbler?" She quickly wiped her hand on her apron and reached for the spatula.

His grin never dimmed. "I sure do. Spent nearly four

hours picking those cherries—I guess I earned a bite or two."

Katy scooped a large serving of the cobbler and slid it onto Jonathan's plate. "There you go. I don't have any whipped cream right now." She gestured toward the kitchen. "Rosemary's whipping up some fresh, so ..."

He leaned his weight on one hip and slipped his free hand into his trouser pocket—the picture of relaxation. "I can wait." Then he stood looking at her, as if he expected her to entertain him.

She wished she could think of something to say, but being in Jonathan's presence left her tongue-tied. So she busied herself rearranging plates and pans that had just been arranged.

"I've been talking with Shelby," Jonathan said.

Katy flicked a glance at him. "Oh?" *Clever, Katy, very clever ...*

"She was telling me about school in Salina." A wistful look came over his face. "It's great that you get to attend. She said you're in Debate."

"Uh-huh." *And don't you sound like a world-class debater right now? Settle down and act normal!*

"I bet it's exciting to compete in tournaments. Shelby said you even won a trophy. I'd like to hear about it sometime, if you don't mind."

Katy ducked her head and tried to form a coherent sentence. "I—I don't mind at all."

"Then maybe—"

"Hey, Katydid, I'll take a slice of apple pie."

Katy jerked her head up at the sound of Caleb's intruding voice.

Caleb thrust his plate at her. "The biggest one."

Why did he have to butt in now? Katy's tongue unloosed. "Caleb Penner, it's exceedingly rude to interrupt and then demand the largest portion. Haven't you ever heard the verse, 'The least shall be first'?" She balled her fist on her hip. "And you *know* I don't like to be called Katydid."

He smirked. "Yeah, I know. That's why I do it." He nudged Jonathan. "Ever wanna get Katy rattled? Call her Katydid. She rises to the bait every time."

Katy proved Caleb right by glowering at him.

Jonathan nudged Caleb back. "Listen, it's not too wise to rattle the woman wielding the dessert spatula. You might not get your pie." He winked at Katy. "Am I right?"

Katy giggled. She waggled the spatula in the air. "You're right."

Caleb sighed. "Okay, okay. Katy, may I have a piece of apple pie?"

See, you can be polite when you want to be. Katy placed a slice of pie—the second-biggest one—on Caleb's plate. "There you are, Caleb." She caught Jonathan's eye, and he grinned. She stifled another giggle.

Caleb eyeballed the pie. "No whipped cream?"

Katy held her hands outward. "All gone."

Caleb frowned. "Pie's better with whipped cream."

"Rosemary made the pie, and it's got lots of cinnamon and sugar," Katy said, pretending sympathy. "You won't miss the whipped cream."

Caleb shuffled off, muttering.

Jonathan watched him go then looked at Katy. "If I didn't know better, I'd say you were trying to get rid of him."

Katy felt her ears heat again. She supposed she hadn't set a very good example, not telling Caleb more whipped cream was coming. Once more she hadn't treated Caleb the way she wanted to be treated. But why did he always seem so determined to irritate her? She couldn't think of a way to respond to Jonathan's comment, so she stood in silence.

Jonathan leaned forward. "I guess you know the reason he teases you so much is because he likes you. He wants your attention, and he's found the way to get it."

Katy huffed. "Well, that's a pretty dumb way to show someone you like her. Why do boys have to act so stupid?" As soon as the words left her mouth, she realized she'd just insulted Jonathan. She slapped her hand over her mouth and gawked at him.

He burst out laughing. "I assume you mean present company excluded?"

Katy nodded rapidly, making her ribbons bounce. She started to apologize, but Rosemary hurried over to the table and plunked a bowl, mounded with frothy whipped cream, on the table. She slipped her arm around Katy's shoulders.

"There you are — that should be enough to take care of any other dessert eaters." She glanced at Jonathan's plate then flashed a quick smile at him. "Did Katy and I do a good job with the cherries?"

"I haven't had a chance to taste the cobbler yet — we've been talking." His gaze whisked from Rosemary to Katy. Katy could have sworn a soft look came over his face when he looked at her. He added, "But I'm sure it'll be great. Especially if you and Katy made it."

Rosemary grinned, giving Katy's shoulders a squeeze. "Well, if you find any pits, you'll have to hold Katy and Shelby responsible — I gave them the deplorable task of pitting the cherries."

Jonathan laughed. "Lucky Katy and Shelby!"

Rosemary whispered in Katy's ear, "If you want to leave your post, I'm sure anyone else who wants dessert can serve himself. Go sit down now and enjoy yourself." She headed back to the kitchen.

Jonathan stood looking at her expectantly. Even though Rosemary had spoken softly, Katy felt certain Jonathan had overheard. He seemed to be waiting for ... something. Then he bounced his plate. "May I have some whipped cream, please?" His eyes glinted with humor.

"Oh!" Katy grabbed the spoon and plopped a huge dollop of cream onto Jonathan's plate.

He grinned. "Thanks, Katy." He backed up a few inches. "There's room at my table, and Shelby's over there, if you ..." He didn't finish the sentence, but she understood.

Katy wanted to go sit at Jonathan's table and visit with him some more. But she had to do something else first. "Thanks. I'll be there in a minute." She picked up the bowl of whipped cream and the apple pie tin and wormed her way through the crowded room to Caleb's table. He'd already finished the slice of pie she'd given him earlier, but he hadn't taken his plate or fork to the kitchen. "Caleb, I've got more whipped cream now. Would you like another piece of pie with some whipped cream on it?"

Caleb's face lit. He held out his plate. "Yeah! Thanks a lot, Katydi — Katy."

She gave him another serving of pie, which she buried

under a mound of whipped cream. When she returned the items to the table, she caught Jonathan's eye. He grinned and nodded, and she knew he approved of her being kind to Caleb. His approval meant as much as Dad's ever had. Her ears heated and the warmth spread into her cheeks. *I'm crushing. I'm majorly crushing.*

Chapter Nine

Dad stepped behind Katy's chair and curled his hands over her shoulders. "Katy, Shelby . . ."

Katy hushed midsentence. Once she'd sat down at his table, Jonathan had asked several questions about the school in Salina, and she'd been telling him about the article she'd had published in a high school literary magazine, *Journalistic Pursuits*, thanks to her English teacher's encouragement. He'd seemed particularly interested. Couldn't Dad have waited just a few more minutes to interrupt the conversation?

"Rosemary's going to stay and help with the kitchen cleanup, but she said you girls should go on home and pack for your overnight stay at Albert and Rebecca's." Dad gave Katy's shoulders a quick pat and then slid his hands into his pockets. "She'll run you to town right after supper. Meet me at the pickup in a few minutes. I need to talk to Albert, and then I'll be out."

"Okay, Dad." Katy retrieved Shelby's crutches from the corner, and when she returned to the table, Jonathan was standing beside Shelby, letting her use his arm to balance herself. Katy's heart turned over in her chest. *He's almost too nice to be real . . .*

Jonathan stayed beside Katy and Shelby all the way from the basement, watching Shelby as she navigated the stairs. Katy thought he'd go back downstairs after he'd escorted them to the top of the stairs, but he grabbed his black, flat-brimmed hat from the rack, placed it on his head, and then walked with them across the yard. Katy's heart pattered. All the Mennonite men wore black hats to church, so she was accustomed to seeing them worn, but somehow the hat made Jonathan appear even more mature and masculine. She had a hard time not staring at him.

They reached Dad's truck, and he opened the door for them. Jonathan took Shelby's crutches, so she slid in first. He placed the crutches in the back while Katy got in. Even then, he didn't leave. Instead, he stood in the door's opening, with one elbow propped on the windowsill and his other hand resting on the top of the truck.

He smiled at Katy, his blue eyes seeming even darker in the shade of his hat's brim. "So . . . what time do you think you'll be heading in to your aunt's house this evening?"

Katy shrugged. "Dad said after supper, but supper might be late tonight. It'll depend on when Rosemary gets home. With a half dozen ladies doing the cleanup, she might be home in an hour. Or it might take longer." She gathered her courage and added, "Why?"

A crooked grin crept up his cheek. "Well, since we don't work on Sunday, it's really my only free day. I was hoping we might get to talk a little more — you know, about school . . . and stuff."

Shelby snickered. Katy gave her a light nudge with her

elbow. "Maybe you could come to my place for supper," Katy said. She quickly amended, "If it's okay with my dad, I mean. I can ask him when he comes out."

Jonathan's smile grew. "That'd be great. But if it'd be too much today—I know you ladies have put in a lot of work for your aunt's luncheon—it's all right. I'll be here 'til the middle of July, at least. We'll have other times to talk."

Katy really wanted to have more time with Jonathan today. *Please let Dad say yes!* The prayer had barely left her heart when Dad emerged from the church building and strode to the pickup. Katy said, "Dad, would it be all right if Jonathan Richter came to our place for supper tonight?" She held her breath.

A funny look came over Dad's face. "Tonight?" He scratched his chin and chuckled. "Probably won't be much of a supper—just leftovers from today's lunch ..."

Katy spun to face Jonathan. "Are leftovers okay with you, Jonathan?"

He shrugged, dropping his hand from the top of the truck to slip it into his pocket. "Leftovers are fine, if you folks don't mind sharing them with me."

Katy quickly turned to give Dad a hopeful look.

Dad shrugged. "All right then. Come by around six."

"Yes, sir!" Jonathan closed the door and shuffled backward, seeming to keep his gaze locked on Katy until Dad pulled the truck out of the parking area.

Dad leaned forward a bit to peek past Shelby at Katy. "Anything you want to tell me, Katy-girl?"

Katy jerked her head to stare out the side window, her ears blazing. "A-about what?"

Dad chuckled. "Never mind."

Shelby giggled.

Katy nudged her.

Shelby nudged Katy back.

Dad chuckled again, but he stayed quiet until they reached the house. When he pulled into the drive, however, he let out a low whistle. "Well, well, well, what's this?"

Katy zinged her gaze forward, and she released a startled gasp. A cherry-red Nova was parked next to the barn. And Bryce sat on its back fender.

❖

For the remainder of the afternoon, Katy's nerves were so on edge she couldn't decide if she would dissolve into hysterical laughter or wild tears. When Dad found out Bryce had been sitting in the hot sun for half an hour, awaiting their return, he insisted Bryce come in for a glass of tea and then invited him to stay for supper. Katy nearly groaned when Bryce accepted.

Two weeks ago if Bryce had shown up unexpectedly at her house, she would have been elated. And a part of her was happy to see him. But why had he come today? She couldn't sit at the supper table with *both* boys and act normal! But how could she gracefully send Bryce away when he'd driven out from Salina?

After issuing the invitation, Dad changed into his work clothes and disappeared into the barn, leaving Katy, Shelby, and Bryce sitting around the kitchen table sipping iced tea. Katy mostly listened to Shelby and Bryce chat. For some reason, she didn't feel like talking.

A little before five, the crunch of gravel alerted them to

someone's arrival. *Jonathan?!* Katy jumped up and dashed to the back door. Her heart sank, and then she mentally scolded herself. *Stop it!* She sent a glance in Shelby's and Bryce's direction. "Rosemary's home ... and Caleb's here too."

Caleb parked by the barn, like always, but Rosemary pulled up beside the back door. Katy gave a little shudder when Caleb hopped out of his car. *I hope Dad doesn't ask Caleb to stay for supper too!* Caleb jogged to the barn, and Rosemary headed for the house. She juggled two casserole dishes and three stacked pie plates. Katy held the door wide for her.

Rosemary looked surprised when she bustled into the kitchen and found Bryce at the table, but she replaced her startled look with a smile. "Well, hello, Bryce. It's nice to see you again." She deposited her armload of containers onto the counter and then crossed to the table for a few minutes, talking with Bryce as easily as if he visited every Sunday afternoon.

Listening, Katy inwardly kicked herself for her mixed feelings. Hadn't she wanted her parents to accept Bryce as her friend so she could possibly spend more time with him? Hadn't she wanted him to feel at ease in her Mennonite community? But now that the things she wanted were happening, she only felt confused.

Because of Jonathan.

Shelby said, "Mr. Lambright asked Bryce to eat with us tonight."

Rosemary beamed. "How nice! We're glad to share a meal with you, Bryce." She turned to Katy. "Since there will be five of us for supper — "

"Six," Shelby said, holding up her fingers to indicate the number. She flashed Katy a grin.

Katy cleared her throat. "Um, Jonathan Richter's coming too."

Rosemary's eyebrows shot up, and so did Bryce's.

"Dad said it was okay," Katy said.

An amused smile creased Rosemary's face. "All right then." She released a soft chuckle. "Since there will be *six* of us for supper, I suggest we eat at the dining room table instead of trying to crowd around the little kitchen table. Katy, would you like to set the table?"

Katy bounced up, grateful for the excuse to leave Bryce's presence for a few minutes yet completely confused by the desire to escape. "Sure." While she put plates, glasses, and silverware on woven placemats, she listened to Shelby, Bryce, and Rosemary visit. The happy sound of their voices, peppered with bursts of laughter, made her heart ache to be a part of the group, but she still prolonged the task to avoid returning to the kitchen. *What is wrong with me?*

When she'd finished setting the table, she chopped vegetables for a tossed salad to go with the leftover potato-and-ham and beef-and-noodle casseroles Rosemary had brought home. The casseroles warmed in the low-heated oven, filling the kitchen with enticing aromas. After everything they'd eaten for lunch, Katy couldn't believe she was hungry, but the good smells made her stomach twist in eagerness to eat again.

Rosemary poured a bag of frozen corn into a saucepan, chuckling. "Potluck for lunch and potluck for supper, but we won't starve." Then she straightened and clapped a hand to her cheek. "Uh-oh!"

"What is it?" Katy asked.

Rosemary waved both hands. "Oh, hardly a calamity, but you know how much your dad likes bread with every meal. I just realized I don't have any. I took every loaf I baked to the luncheon, and there wasn't a single slice left over." She stuck her head in the pantry and then emerged, frowning. "No rolls, either. I guess your dad will have to do without bread for supper."

Bryce said, "I'd be glad to run into town and buy a loaf real quick."

Rosemary laughed. "Well, I suppose that's an option in Salina, but our little grocery in Schellberg is never open on Sundays—it's the Lord's day, you know."

"Oh. Sorry." Bryce slunk low in his chair.

Rosemary sent a crinkling smile in Bryce's direction. "Now, don't wilt on me. If it were Saturday or Monday, I'd give Katy my car keys and send her straight to town. But ..." She held her hands outward. "Not today."

"I could mix up some baking soda biscuits," Katy said. She glanced at the wall clock—twenty 'til six. "There's time yet if I hurry." Mixing, rolling, and cutting biscuit dough would keep her busy too, so she wouldn't have to think.

"But is there room in the oven for a baking sheet with those casserole dishes in there?" Rosemary cracked the door and peeked inside. She straightened, shaking her head. "I'd have to take one of the dishes out, and then we'd have a cold casserole." She wrinkled her nose. "No, he'll just have to do without bread tonight. I'm sure we'll have enough to eat between the casseroles, salad, corn, and leftover pies. But just in case ..." She began rummaging in the refrigerator, removing jars of home-pickled cucumbers and beets and store-bought olives.

Katy opened a cabinet door to get out small serving bowls for the various condiments, and someone knocked on the front door. She sent Rosemary a startled look. "I wonder who that is." No one from Schellberg ever came to the front door — everyone used the back door, since the driveway was behind the house.

Rosemary peeked over the top of the refrigerator door and frowned. "I hope it isn't some sort of salesman. Not on *Sunday.*" Quite often salesmen peddling wares related to dairy farming showed up uninvited to try and tempt Dad with newer machinery and conveniences.

"I'll find out." Katy clacked the bowls onto the counter and hurried to the front door. She had to twist the sticky, seldom-used lock before she could open the door, and when she swung it wide, she found Jonathan Richter on the porch, still dressed in his Sunday trousers, white shirt, and suit jacket. He held one hand behind his back, and the other pressed his black hat against his stomach. The pose made him look very formal and grown up.

"Hi, Katy. I hope I'm not too early." He tipped his head and smiled. "Your dad said six, so ..."

"It's just fine. Come on in." She felt out of breath. Probably from her mad dash to the front door. *Uh-huh, right* ... Stepping backward, she gave him room to enter the house.

He crossed the threshold and then stood just inside the door, smiling at her. He brought his hand from behind his back and dangled a plastic sack stuffed with crusty rolls. "I hope you can use these."

Katy gawked at the sack. "How did you know ...?" But of course he didn't know — it was just a coincidence. Even so, having him provide the one thing their meal lacked made Katy's pulse zip into overdrive.

"Sandra sent them," he said, referring to his cousin's wife. "She forgot to take them to the church this morning, and she baked way too many for just Dan, Sandra, and me."

Katy took the bag and hugged it against her front. "Thank you." She flapped her hand at the standing coat-rack beside the door. "You can put your coat and hat on the rack there." She waited until he followed her instructions, noting how he smoothed the fabric of his coat after hanging it rather than just slopping it onto a hook. She appreciated the care he took with his belongings.

Realizing she was staring, she gave herself a little shake. "Come on back to the kitchen and have a seat." She led him through the dining room toward the kitchen. She gestured to the neatly set table as they passed it. "We don't have dinner on the table yet because Dad is still out in the barn with the cows. We'll have to wait until he's finished, but it shouldn't be much longer. As Dad said, it'll just be leftovers, but — " She was rambling. She closed her mouth with a snap.

They entered the kitchen, and Bryce jumped to his feet. Jonathan came to a halt right inside the kitchen and his gaze seemed to collide with Bryce's. The two boys faced each other, neither smiling.

Shelby looked back and forth between Bryce and Jonathan several times before shifting to look at Katy. Amusement glinted in her eyes. She cleared her throat.

"Hi, Jonathan. You remember Bryce from Annika's party? He's eating here tonight too."

"Hi, Bryce." Jonathan spoke politely, but he didn't smile. "Good to see you again."

Bryce gave a brusque nod. "Hi."

Katy scurried to Rosemary's side, ready to whisper a request for her to play hostess and *quick*! But before she could say a word, the back door flew open and Dad stepped through.

Dad paused, sent a glance across everyone, then his face broke into a wide smile. He rubbed his hands together. "Good! Everyone's here. Let me wash up, and we can eat." He headed for the sink, giving Katy a surreptitious wink on the way.

Katy balled her hands into fists and inwardly growled. Dad was having way too much fun!

Chapter Ten

Katy tucked the cover under Trent's chin. "Now you take a nice long nap, and when you wake up, I'll have a special treat ready for you."

The little boy yawned. "'Kay, Katy." He pulled his ratty stuffed dog to his cheek, poked his thumb into his mouth, and closed his eyes.

Katy crept out of the room, relieved that her youngest cousin gave in so easily. The morning had been hectic with the boys—ages three, seven, and nine—running wild and the fourteen-year-old twins, Lori and Lola, constantly scolding them or arguing with each other. Katy understood that her cousins were upset and worried about their mom so she tried to be patient. But she was ready for a break.

She entered the living room and found Lori and Lola slumped side by side on the sofa. Shelby sat nearby in Uncle Albert's overstuffed chair. It was quiet. Way too quiet. Katy looked around in confusion. "Where are Benji and Mark?"

Lori waved her hand in the direction of the front door. "Mrs. Krehbiel came by and offered to take them to her house to play with her boys this afternoon." She heaved a huge sigh. "So we get some peace and quiet."

"Thank goodness," Lola added, snuggling a little lower on the sofa. "I might do like Trent and take a nap. I didn't sleep very good last night."

Sleep very well. Katy considered correcting Lola's grammar but thought better of it. She didn't want to incite another argument. "That's understandable," she said, using her most soothing tone. "I tell you what." She plucked her purse from the floor beside the sofa and withdrew her billfold. "Why don't you and Lori walk to the café and have a milkshake ... on me?"

Lola sat straight up. "Really?"

Lori licked her lips. "That sounds great."

Katy said, "I promised Trent a treat if he'd take an extra-long nap, so maybe you could bring home a brownie for him." She removed a ten-dollar bill from her billfold. "Get one for Benji and Mark too."

Lori bounced up and took the bill from Katy's hand. "Thanks!" The pair dashed out the door, their cap ribbons flitting over their shoulders.

The moment they left, Katy plopped into the middle of the sofa and blew out a mighty breath. "Ahh, *now* we've got peace and quiet."

Shelby grinned. "It has been pandemonium, hasn't it?"

Katy nodded in agreement, her eyebrows high. "But," she admitted on a sigh, "it's been kind of a relief too."

"Oh, yeah? How so?"

Katy almost wished she'd kept her thought to herself.

Shelby might start teasing her again, but she'd opened the door to the conversation — she might as well walk through it. "When I'm busy, I don't think. And thinking about Bryce and Jonathan wears me out."

To Shelby's credit, she didn't giggle. But she did smirk. A little. "Ah. Gotcha."

Katy sat up and propped her elbows on her knees. "It was so weird yesterday evening, having them both at the table, both looking at me, both wanting my attention ... Can you say, 'awkward'?"

Shelby still didn't laugh. "I know. I felt kind of sorry for you." She lifted one shoulder in a lopsided shrug. "But, honestly, Katy, what a problem to have. Most girls would kill to be the target of affection from two awesome guys."

Katy blinked. "You really think they're both awesome?"

Shelby snorted. "Duh!"

The girls sat in silence for a few seconds, and then Katy asked, "Shelby, have you ever liked two boys at the same time?"

"Well, sure," Shelby said quickly. She draped her cast-covered foot over the armrest of the chair. "I mean, it's not that unusual to crush on several guys." She released a soft laugh. "Of course, I've never had the pleasure of multiple guys crushing on me at the same time ..."

Katy made a face. "You make it sound like it's some sort of privilege, but really, it's just uncomfortable. Especially since ..." She bit down on her lower lip.

Shelby sat up, fixing Katy with an interested look. "Especially since ... what?"

Katy hung her head. "Since neither of them are really a good choice for me."

"Are you kidding me?" Shelby's voice burst out two decibels higher than usual. "Katy, how could either of them not be perfect? They're both really nice, they're both really good-looking, and they're both crazy about you. Any girl would be nuts not to dive into a relationship with either of them!"

Katy met Shelby's gaze. "But I'm not any girl. I'm a Mennonite who lives in Schellberg, Kansas."

"So?"

A little huff of frustration left Katy's throat. "Shelby, think about it. Would Bryce join my faith to be with me? Would Jonathan leave his family in Lancaster County to be with me? For me to have a relationship with either of them, I have to face the possibility of leaving my home — something I don't want to do! How can that make them right for me?"

Shelby crinkled her nose. "Katy ..."

Katy hurried on. "It would break my dad's heart if I left the Mennonite faith to be with Bryce." *My mom leaving nearly killed him.* "And what about being with Jonathan? I've heard Rosemary talk about how much she misses her daughter who married a man from Ohio." *I'm the only kid Dad has.* Her nose stung as tears threatened. "No matter who I'd choose, it would be wrong. So I need to stop liking them."

Shelby shook her head. The short layers of hair around her face wisped across her cheeks with the motion. "Back up a minute. I think you're being too serious. You just turned seventeen at the beginning of the summer! It's way too soon to be thinking about being with someone *permanently.*" She flipped her hands outward. "Why can't you just go out with one of them — or even both of them — and have some fun?"

Because that's not how it's done in my community. Katy kept the comment to herself. Group activities were fine, but pairing up sent a completely different message within the fellowship. Shelby wouldn't understand how many of the girls from her fellowship became published to be married at ages not much older than Katy. Her own mother was only eighteen when she'd married Dad and twenty-one when Katy was born. For her Old Order Mennonite sect, seventeen meant being finished with school, possessing the skills to be a wife and mother, and being considered mature enough to enter into a marriage relationship.

She said, "It doesn't work that way for me."

"Well," Shelby said in a reasonable tone, "then I guess the best thing to do is let both of them know right now you aren't interested. Or they'll be like Caleb — showing up every time you turn around." Her eyes grew round and she whistled softly. "I can't believe Bryce just came out on Sunday. And it's obvious Jonathan wants time with you. But if you really think spending time with either of them will lead to you being pulled away from your dad and your town, then you gotta just tell them ... 'don't come around.'"

Katy folded her arms over her chest and huffed again. "That's easier to talk about than actually do."

Shelby laughed. "Yeah, I know, but — " The telephone in her pocket started playing a tune. She yanked it out and flipped it open. She looked at the little screen, and a funny smile curved her lips. She clicked the *on* button and put the phone to her ear. "Hi, Bryce."

Katy's heart jumped into her throat.

Shelby listened for a moment, her forehead furrowed, and then she grinned. "Yeah, she's right here."

Katy waved her hands wildly, shaking her head so hard her ribbons flopped.

But Shelby held the phone out to Katy and whispered, "Here's your chance—set him straight."

Katy's hand trembled as she took the telephone from Shelby and pressed it to her ear. "H-hi, Bryce."

"Katy ..." His familiar voice carried clearly through the line. "Thanks again for supper last night. I know I kind of barged in on you, but it was great to be included."

Katy swallowed. She wanted to tell him it was great to see him too, but she was afraid the words wouldn't be completely true. "You're welcome."

For several seconds neither of them spoke. Then Bryce's voice blasted. "Part of the reason I came out yesterday was to ask you about something. But then other people"—somehow Katy knew he meant Jonathan—"were there, and it just didn't seem right to ask."

Katy clutched the little phone with both hands. "What's that?" She wished her voice would sound normal instead of squeaking.

"Well, the youth group at my church is getting together this coming Saturday. We're doing a sand volleyball tournament at the park. And then I thought we could go get a pizza or something afterward. Just you and me." The final sentence communicated the purpose of his call. He was asking her on a date.

Katy's heart set up a wild thudding that made her breath come in little spurts. "Bryce, I ..." She gulped, and tears stung behind her nose. She liked Bryce so much.

But as she'd just told Shelby, they came from two different worlds. Praying silently for the right words, she bravely pressed on. "I really appreciate you asking me. And I know I'd have fun. But I think ... I think I need to say no."

Another lengthy silence hung on the line. Then Bryce's voice again. Soft, and uncertain. "Oh. Well ..."

The hurt in his voice pierced Katy. "I'm sorry. It's just that dating is taken pretty seriously around here. If I went out with you — just you and me, alone — people would think ..." Bryce was smart enough to understand without her spelling it all out.

"Yeah. I see what you're saying." He still sounded hurt, but at least he wasn't angry. "I guess it's not such a great idea after all."

"But that doesn't mean I don't want to be your friend," Katy blurted. "You — you're special to me, Bryce. You, and Shelby and Cora and Trisha ... I don't know what I'd do without you at school." She caught Shelby's eye, and Shelby gave an encouraging nod. Katy continued. "Even if we don't ... date ... we can still talk and — and ..."

"And be debate partners?"

Katy smiled, hugging the phone to her cheek. He wasn't mad, and he wasn't throwing her friendship aside. "Yes. I'd really like that."

Another time of silence fell, but this one wasn't awkward. It felt more like a settling in, of finding a comfortable niche. Katy waited for Bryce to speak again.

"Well, I guess I should let you go then."

Katy swallowed a lump of sadness. His words held a double meaning, although he probably didn't realize it. "Yeah ..."

"I'll keep your aunt in my prayers. You and Shelby have fun. I'll talk to you later." A little *click* disconnected the line.

Katy held the phone for a few more seconds, blinking to hold back tears. Tears of both regret and relief.

"You okay?" Shelby asked.

Shelby's sympathetic tone increased Katy's desire to cry, but she sniffed hard and nodded. She handed the phone back. "I'm okay. I did the right thing." *I just wish doing the right thing didn't have to be so hard sometimes.*

Chapter Eleven

For the remainder of the week, Katy stayed too busy to think much about Bryce or Jonathan. Aunt Rebecca came home from the hospital on Thursday afternoon, but Uncle Albert wouldn't allow her to step foot out of the house, leaving Katy and Shelby to run the shop alone. Katy didn't mind — she'd worked summers and Saturdays in the fabric shop since she was thirteen, so she was familiar with the routine, and the last few weeks with Shelby had gone well. But being in charge was very different from following her aunt's directions. Even though things went smoothly, she still felt exhausted from the weight of responsibility.

Saturday noon she put the CLOSED sign into place and then sank onto the window ledge with a mighty sigh. "Oh, wow, I am *sooo* looking forward to the weekend!"

Shelby grabbed her crutches and hobbled to Katy. "It should be a quiet one, since you won't be going to that volleyball tourney with Bryce."

Guilt pinched the corners of Katy's heart as she thought about her conversation with Bryce. Although she'd been honest, she still felt very bad. She never enjoyed hurting someone's feelings, especially when she cared about the person as much as she cared about Bryce.

"Unless, of course, Jonathan makes an appearance at the house."

Katy turned her head in Shelby's direction. "Why would he do that? I mean, he only came out last Sunday because I invited him. I don't think he'd be forward enough to just ... well ... *show up*." She turned her attention to a hangnail on her thumb. "Besides, he's working for his cousin. Corn harvest is right around the corner — I'm sure Dan Richter will keep Jonathan plenty busy." Until that moment, she didn't realize how much she'd missed Jonathan during the week. She pushed away the beginnings of melancholy and asked, "Since we have the afternoon free, what do you want to do?"

Shelby tipped her head. "Should we go by your aunt's house and give her an update on how things have gone here? I'm sure she'd like to know."

Katy nodded. "Great idea. Let me do one more check to make sure everything's in order, and then we'll go."

When Katy and Shelby entered the house, they found Aunt Rebecca stretched out on the sofa. Katy released a little gasp. She'd never seen her aunt without a cap covering her hair. But today Aunt Rebecca's long dark hair, woven with a few silvery strands, hung across the bodice of her cotton robe. She looked years younger. And very fragile and vulnerable. Tears stung the back of Katy's nose.

Katy sat gingerly on the edge of the sofa. "We just wanted to come by and see if you had any questions ... about the shop." She forced a bright smile. "Things went well, but we missed you."

Aunt Rebecca offered a tired smile. "It's nice to be missed. I hope to be in some next week. I'm still a little worn out from the surgery, but each day I feel stronger. I won't have another chemo treatment until a week from Monday, so the next few days should be better."

Shelby hitched to the end of the sofa. "While we're here, do you need help with anything? Dishes washed? Laundry?"

Katy hadn't thought about asking the question. She flashed a grin in Shelby's direction, grateful for her consideration. "Yes. We could — "

"No, no," Aunt Rebecca said, shaking her head slowly. "The twins are very capable of handling the household chores, and your gramma Ruthie is keeping the boys under control." She sighed. "They've been especially rowdy, but I suppose I can't blame them. Their world has been disrupted."

Again, Katy was struck by the change in Aunt Rebecca's attitude. She'd never been one to tolerate any kind of misbehavior. Yet, as sick as she must feel, she chose to exhibit patience and understanding rather than frustration. Katy squeezed her aunt's knee through the robe. "Yours has been too."

Aunt Rebecca chuckled softly then sighed. "I suppose. But it's given me a chance to slow down and reflect. Sometimes that's a good thing for a person to do." Her expression turned pensive.

Katy wasn't sure how to respond, so she stood. "Well, we'll get out of your way so you can rest. We'll see you in service on Sunday?"

Aunt Rebecca shook her head slightly. "I doubt it, Katy.

Albert prefers I stay in for a full week after my release from the hospital. So I probably won't see you again until the middle of next week when I come into the shop ... unless you stop by here."

Katy wondered if her aunt meant to hint she should come by. She smiled. "Maybe we'll all come by after service Sunday. We can check on you and bring you a special treat. Rosemary always bakes something good on Saturday for Sunday's dessert, so — "

Aunt Rebecca grimaced. "Nothing rich, please. My stomach ..." She pressed both hands to her middle. "It isn't tolerating food very well right now."

"All right. Just a visit then. And if you're not up to it, you can just send us all away."

Her aunt smiled — a genuine, tender smile. "That's sweet, Katy. You girls enjoy your time off. Do something fun."

"We will." Katy ushered Shelby to the door. "'Bye now."

Out under the smoldering sun again, Katy blew out a huge breath. "Wow ... Aunt Rebecca isn't Aunt Rebecca anymore."

"Yeah, she looks really weak and worn out," Shelby said.

Katy frowned. "Yes, but that's not what I meant. There's something ... different."

Shelby paused beside the cart, balancing on her crutches. "How so?"

Katy glanced toward the house, various images of her aunt playing through her mind — remembrances from the past competing with the present. "She doesn't *act* like herself. It's weird, Shelby." She helped Shelby climb into the two-wheeled cart as she explained, "All my life, I've felt like I needed to be careful about what I said or did around my aunt. She can be so critical and picky. But now ..." Katy boosted herself onto the seat and picked up the reins. "She's actually kind of ..." She sought a word.

"Nice?" Shelby contributed.

Katy flicked the reins, and the cart jolted forward. Shelby's choice was too simplistic, but it worked. "Yes. Nice." She sent Shelby a sidelong look. "And you're right about her looking really, really tired. I wonder how long it'll be before she's able to take care of the shop again."

Shelby shrugged. "Cancer isn't something you just get over in a week or so. She'll probably be sick for as long as she takes chemo."

"That'll be weeks — maybe months," Katy mused.

Shelby grabbed Katy's arm. "Katy, what about school? I mean, if she's still not feeling strong enough to run the fabric store when mid-August arrives and school starts up again, what will you do? Will you find someone else to work in the shop so you can go to school, or will you have to drop out?"

For the first time, Katy realized her aunt's illness might affect more than just her summer. She gulped.

Katy turned to Shelby. "Well, how about — "

"Katy!"

The male voice brought Katy's comment to an abrupt halt. She turned and spotted Caleb jogging toward her. Pulling on the reins to stop Rocky, she sucked in a breath of fortification, reminding herself she needed to be *nice* no matter what Caleb wanted.

He caught up to the girls and flashed a freckled smile

over both of them. "Hey, you got anything planned for this afternoon?"

Shelby opened her mouth to answer, but Katy cut her off. "Why?"

"A bunch of us are gettin' together and driving to the bowling alley in Salina."

Shelby's eyebrows shot up. "You *bowl?*"

Katy laughed at Shelby's surprise. "Yes, the young people often go into Salina to bowl or go roller skating. Those are favorite activities, especially during the winter when there isn't much else to do."

Caleb glanced at Shelby's cast and grimaced. "I guess you wouldn't be able to actually bowl, but maybe you could cheer us on or something. That is, if you girls wanna join us."

Katy and Shelby exchanged a look. Katy read the desire in Shelby's eyes to get away and do something. She said, "Sounds all right. I'll have to check with Dad first, and he'll want to know who all is going."

Caleb rolled his eyes skyward and crunched his face in concentration. He flicked his fingers in the air as he named young people from Schellberg. "Um, lemme see ... Annika, Todd, Justin, I think maybe your cousins Lori and Lola if their dad says yes, Jane and Terry, Yvonne — oh." He made a face. "I s'pose that means her cousin Jonathan'll go too. She seems to drag him everywhere."

Katy wanted to smack Caleb for his derisive tone. What was his problem with Jonathan?

Shelby whistled. "Wow, that's quite a few kids. How are you all getting there?"

Caleb shrugged. "Todd and me both have cars that'll

hold six people if we squeeze three into the front seats."
His grin twitched. "You and Katy could ride with me."

"I need to check with Dad," Katy repeated. "If we do
go, we'll drive ourselves and meet you there. You go on
ahead."

"Better hurry. I've gotta go pick up my riders right now."

"What about lunch?" Shelby asked. She rubbed her
stomach. "I'm hungry."

Katy was too. The store had been busy all morning, and
the macaroni and cheese casserole Rosemary had promised them for lunch was sounding better by the minute.

"We're gonna eat at the bowling alley," Caleb said.
"They've got that grill where they cook burgers or hot
dogs."

Katy had eaten at the bowling alley before. Caleb might
appreciate their food, but she thought everything was
greasy and flavorless. "Yuck."

Caleb shook his head and huffed. "Fine, then eat at
home first if you want. Do you think your dad will let you
go or not? We need to know whether to wait at the bowling alley for you."

Katy wished she knew for sure if Jonathan was going.
He probably had to work all Saturday afternoon. "I don't
know, Caleb. Like I said, I'll have to check with my dad.
And I'm not sure I want to spend money for bowling ..."

Caleb huffed again. "All right, but don't say you didn't
have the chance to do something fun." He whirled and
charged off toward his car.

Shelby lightly bopped Katy on the leg. "What's the
deal? Other than going to the sundae party at Annika's, all
you've done since I got here is work at the fabric shop or

hang out at your house. I've got some money — I could've paid for us to go." She looked longingly toward Caleb's car as it rolled out of town. "They could have saved room for us, if you'd said yes."

Guilt pricked. Although Katy wasn't keen on spending the afternoon with Caleb, she didn't want to spoil any potential fun for Shelby. Shelby probably felt stifled, stuck here in Schellberg away from all her other friends. If they went to Salina, Shelby could call Trisha and Cora. Maybe they'd come to the bowling alley and play a couple of games too.

"I'm sorry, Shelby," Katy said, and she meant it. She loosened the reins and urged Rocky forward. "Want me to see if Dad will let me borrow the truck and drive to Salina after lunch? He's let me take it twice before."

Shelby's grin returned. "That'd be great. No offense, but I'm a little stir-crazy. I'm not used to small towns and cows for company. I'd love to just get out and *do* something." Then she laughed. "Not that I can do much with this crazy plaster-covered foot. But even doing nothing somewhere else would be kind of nice."

At lunch, Dad looked uncertain when Katy asked permission to take the truck into Salina, but Rosemary leaned forward and put her hand on his arm. "Now, Samuel, these girls have worked extra hard for the past two weeks. Don't you think they deserve a little diversion? If you're reluctant to let Katy use the truck, I'd be willing to give up my car. I won't need it this afternoon, so it's fine with me." Then she added in her typical diplomatic way, "But it's up to you."

Katy gave Dad her best pleading look. Driving Rosemary's car was preferable to driving Dad's old truck anyway. The car was not only more comfortable, it had an automatic transmission, making it much easier to drive.

Dad worked his jaw back and forth for a few seconds. He fiddled with his fork and pushed some macaroni around his plate. Finally he sighed. "Well, I suppose it's all right — "

Shelby let out a little squeal, and Katy grinned.

" — if you're extra careful." He softened his stern look when he turned to Rosemary. "The bowling alley's on the edge of town, right off the highway. So she won't have to do much busy in-town driving."

Katy cringed. Did Dad have to embarrass her that way? She knew how to drive!

"I'm sure she'll do fine," Rosemary said. "Girls, you are welcome to take my car. And you'd better hurry, or you might not be able to join your friends in time."

Katy grinned, overcome by Rosemary's generous and trusting offer of her car. She wished she could give Rosemary a big hug of thanks, but for some reason it still felt funny offering spontaneous hugs to her stepmother. *Maybe if Aunt Rebecca can make such major changes, I can too.* She'd have to give that idea further thought later on.

Shelby asked, "Is it okay if I call Cora and Trisha and ask if they can join us? We haven't seen them in weeks."

"Of course," Katy said. "I was going to suggest it myself."

A grin spread across Shelby's face. "Afternoon of fun, here we come!"

While Shelby called their friends, Katy changed into a lightweight floral dress and put on brown sandals in place of her tennis shoes. She tucked a pair of socks in her purse, though, to wear with the bowling shoes then made her way down the stairs. But once she reached the bottom, someone knocked on the front door.

"Oh no," Shelby groaned, "not now. We're supposed to be getting out of here!"

Katy crunched her lips into a sympathetic grimace. "Let me check to see who's here. If it's a sales call I'll get Dad. Then we can go."

Shelby sighed and shuffled toward the kitchen.

Katy skipped to the front door, gave the lock a fierce twist, and swung the door open. But once again no salesman stood on the porch. Instead, she looked into the smiling face of Jonathan Richter.

Chapter Twelve

"H-hi, Jonathan," Katy said, trying not to sound as surprised as she felt. From now on, every time someone knocked on the front door, she would think of Jonathan. Her heart fluttered at the realization.

"Hi. I'm sorry to barge in on you unannounced, but I've got the afternoon free, and — "

Shelby limped up beside Katy, impatience marring her brow. "Oh. Hi, Jonathan."

Jonathan bounced a smile at her. "Hi, Shelby. I was just telling Katy, I've got the afternoon free, and I thought I'd go out to the pasture and spend an hour or so with Saydee and Shadow." He turned to Katy again. "But I wanted to ask your permission first."

Katy clung to the edge of the door, wishing her pulse would slow down. Why did it tend to gallop whenever Jonathan came around? This boy was too appealing. "S-sure, I told you before — feel free to spend as much time as you want with them."

"Great." He smiled, his whole face lighting. He raised one eyebrow. "Are you going to be out there at all today?"

He sounded so hopeful. Katy gulped. Oh, how she wanted to say yes! But she'd promised Shelby a trip to Salina. "I doubt it. We're going bowling. In Salina. Shelby got a hold of a couple of our high school friends to see if they can join us — kind of have a girls' time, you know?"

His eyebrows twitched downward and then back into place. "No Bryce? He's — from Salina too, right?"

Katy nodded then shook her head. "He's from Salina, but we aren't calling him ... today." A strange twinge of disappointment coiled through her chest. Shouldn't she long to see Bryce even if she'd decided she needed to back off?

"Oh." Jonathan offered a quick nod. "Yvonne went with Justin and some of the others. She asked me, but ..." His grin turned sheepish. "I'm not very good at bowling. I'd probably hurt somebody."

Shelby said, "That's too bad. Might've been fun, but I'm sure you'll enjoy your time with the horses." She waved. "Well, we'll see you later, Jonathan." She turned and stumped quickly toward the kitchen.

Katy gawked after her. Had Shelby intended to be rude? She faced Jonathan and lifted her shoulders in an apologetic shrug. "I guess Shelby's ready to go, so ..."

Jonathan grinned and slapped his bill cap over his tousled blond hair. "Have a good time. Thanks for letting me hang out with your horses." He turned and bounded off the porch.

Katy closed the door and hurried after Shelby, who waited beside the back door. "Shelby! What is with you? You basically dismissed him!"

"I'm sorry if I came off as uncivil." Shelby didn't look

sorry at all. "But I was just trying to help you out. You said it wouldn't work for you to be in a relationship with Jonathan, but every time he comes around, you get all ... I don't know ... kind of soft and goofy. You don't have any willpower where he's concerned."

As much as Katy wanted to, she couldn't deny Shelby's assessment. Being around Jonathan did funny things to her stomach. She just hadn't realized it showed. She'd need to watch herself.

"So I figured I'd help you out by sending him to the horses." Shelby tipped her head to the side. "If you want, we can just take the horse cart out to the pasture instead of going bowling."

For a moment, Katy was tempted to do as Shelby suggested. But hadn't she decided she should stay away from Jonathan? And Shelby really wanted to go to town. Plus she'd already asked Cora and Trisha to meet them at the bowling alley. She sighed. "No, Dad gave us permission to go to town, so we're going."

"You sure?"

Katy nodded emphatically. "I'm sure." She grabbed her little purse from its hook by the back door and hurried Shelby outside before she changed her mind.

✛

Katy swung her arm and released the sparkly blue ball she'd chosen from the rack because it reminded her of Jonathan's sparkling eyes. Behind her, Shelby, Cora, and Trisha cheered as the ball curved toward the gutter then swerved back to center. The ball careened into the triangle of red-striped white pins, and they crashed and spun. Katy

held her breath—would she get a strike? But when everything settled, two pins in the far left corner remained.

"Awww!" she groused, but she smiled.

"You can pick 'em up, Katy," Cora said, clapping wildly.
"Get your spare!"

Katy flashed a grin over her shoulder. "I'll do my best!"

Although she'd experienced some apprehensions about
coming, she was having a great time with her Salina
friends. The Schellberg kids occupied the two lanes to
Katy's right, so she was a part of their group too. Sort of.

Her ball returned, and she scooped it from the tray.
Poised, she envisioned the course the ball would take, then
stepped up and let it fly. It hit neatly between the two pins,
sending them both off the lane. A spare! Katy jumped up
and down and clapped while Trisha, Cora, and Shelby
erupted in whoops. Smiling, Katy turned to skip back to
the bench, but Caleb reached across the little divider between lanes.

He stuck his hand in the air, palm out. "Great shot,
Katy!"

After a moment's hesitation, Katy clapped palms with
him.

He pointed at the scoreboard above the lanes. "Look at
that! You're two pins ahead of me."

Katy would have expected him to pout about her being
ahead—Caleb tended to be competitive when it came to
games—but instead he seemed pleased.

Then he smirked. "'Course, the game's not over yet."

Katy scowled at him. "I'll stay ahead, Caleb. Just wait
and see!"

"Yeah!" Shelby turned backward on the bench and gave

Caleb an exaggerated snarl. "My girl Katy here is gonna *stomp* you." Cora and Trisha added their good-natured taunts.

Caleb threw a challenging look across the group. "Oh yeah? Well, how about this? Loser buys the winner ice cream." He folded his arms over his chest and grinned at Katy. "Willing to back up your talk with action?"

What Caleb suggested was a bet, and Katy knew Dad would frown if she participated in even a friendly bet. But before she could refuse, Shelby piped up, "You're on."

Caleb laughed and stepped up to the lane. In three smooth steps, he reached the line and rolled the ball. Katy sucked in her breath as the ball seemed to slide halfway down the lane. Then it began to whirl. A mighty *crash!* erupted when it plowed into the pins. They flew, bouncing into each other, and not a single one remained standing. He turned to the girls and bowed. They groaned, but he just laughed.

"Lucky shot," Shelby teased, and Caleb laughed again. He plunked onto the bench and continued smirking at Katy.

Katy sat beside Shelby while Cora and Trisha took their turns. Shelby nudged Katy and whispered, "Caleb's been a lot of fun today."

Katy grimaced, but she nodded. Even though he'd done some teasing, it hadn't been mean-spirited but playful. She'd actually enjoyed sparring with him. Annika had even joined in, sometimes siding with Caleb, sometimes siding with Katy. Cora and Trisha had added their sassy comments, and they'd all done more laughing than Katy could remember doing in a long time. It felt really good—

comfortable — to be having fun with all her friends at the same time.

In the last frame, Katy managed a spare followed by four pins, but Caleb got a strike and then a spare. He ended up beating Katy by six pins.

He punched the air with his fist and whooped. "Ha! Gotcha!" He waggled his eyebrows. "I knew I would."

"Aw, you just got lucky there at the end," Cora insisted, sending a fierce scowl across the divider at Caleb.

"Not luck," Caleb insisted, "self-preservation. If I lost, I'd have to buy all of you" — he swung his arm to indicate Katy and all three of her friends — "ice cream. I'd've gone broke!"

Katy shook her head, and the others groaned.

Trisha said, "Challenge round! Give Katy another chance. I know she'll skunk you."

"Can't be a next round." Caleb sounded genuinely disappointed. "We only prepaid for two rounds, and we're done." He gestured to people standing in the waiting area. "Gotta give the lanes over to others."

With sad mutters, everyone sat down and pulled off their bowling shoes. Minutes later, they ambled into the parking lot in one big mob of kids with Katy and Caleb in the middle of the throng.

Caleb sent Katy an impish grin before raising his voice and addressing everyone. "Hey! Who's up for ice cream?"

Cheers arose.

"How about Braum's?" Annika suggested.

"Nah, the booths at Braum's are too small," one of the older boys said. "There's a Cold Stone Creamery in the mall. Let's go there — we can pull tables together in the food court and all sit together."

Several kids, including Annika, offered their agreement.

Caleb nudged Katy with his elbow. "Got your money ready? I'm probably gonna want the biggest bowl they've got." He rubbed his stomach and grinned. "I worked up an appetite besting you."

Katy rolled her eyes, but she couldn't stop a grin from forming. Since when was Caleb so charming? "You'll have to be satisfied with a small bowl — that's all I have funds for. Besides, you didn't beat me by *that* much. Six pins hardly warrants a large-sized bowl."

Caleb laughed loudly and began backpedaling. "Okay, Katydid, a small bowl. See ya there." He spun and caught up to the others, who waited beside his car.

Shelby limped up beside Katy and gave her a speculative look. "Hmm ..."

Katy crunched her eyebrows. "Hmm, what?"

Shelby's lips twitched. "Caleb Penner just called you 'Katydid,' and you didn't even flinch. What's up with that?"

Cora and Trisha giggled. Cora jiggled Katy's arm. "Yeah, Katy, how come you never mentioned how cute some of the boys from Schellberg are? Trisha and I might have to come shopping for boyfriends in your town." They giggled again.

Katy scowled and headed for Rosemary's car. "C'mon, you guys. Caleb's not cute."

They scurried after her, Shelby bringing up the rear with her crutches. Cora said, "You're kidding, right? He *is* cute, Katy. How could you not think his ruffled hair

and freckles aren't adorable? I mean, he looks enough
like Bryce to be his brother, and you think Bryce is cute,
right?"

Katy stared at Cora. She'd often noticed similarities in
appearance between the two boys, but Caleb had never
measured up. Mostly because of his behavior. He was so
irritating most of the time. But today he hadn't irritated
her. Her ears started to heat.

She jammed the key into the door lock, turned it, and
then opened the door. "It's hard to think of Caleb as cute. I
know him too well. And he's been a major pest ever since
we started school together."

Trisha shrugged. "People can change. He seemed nice
enough to me."

"To me too," Cora said with a sigh. "Makes me wish we
could join you at the mall, but I have to have my mom's
car back by four thirty. So we don't have time."

The girls exchanged hugs and said their good-byes.
Katy helped Shelby into the passenger seat then tossed the
crutches into the back. She pulled carefully into traffic and
aimed the car for the mall. From the other side of the seat,
Shelby suddenly gasped.

Katy shot her a startled look. "What?"

Shelby waved both hands, grimacing. "Nothing. Never
mind."

Curiosity teased Katy. Keeping her eyes on traffic, she
said, "No, really. What?"

Shelby shifted sideways a bit to catch the corner of
Katy's eyes. "If I tell you, promise you won't get mad?"

Katy couldn't imagine getting mad at Shelby. She was
too easygoing. "I promise."

"Okay then ..." Shelby sucked in a long breath and released it in a whoosh. "I was just thinking about you needing to avoid seeing Bryce or Jonathan because they might pull you away from Schellberg or your dad."

Katy nodded slowly. For reasons she couldn't understand, her heart began to thud.

"I mean, Bryce isn't Mennonite, and Jonathan's from Pennsylvania ..."

Katy sent Shelby an impatient glance. "Okay, so ...?"

"Well, it just occurred to me. There is a guy in Schellberg who can be pretty cool when he wants to be. And he obviously likes you. And since he's both a Mennonite *and* a Schellberg resident, there'd be no chance of him pulling you away from either your faith or your family, so—"

Katy let out a little screech of protest. "Don't say it!" The light turned red. Katy jammed on the brakes. Both she and Shelby jolted with the sudden stop. Her hands curling tightly around the steering wheel, she glared at Shelby. "Just because we had one pleasant afternoon doesn't mean I want to be courted by Caleb Penner!"

Shelby held her hands out in defeat. "You promised not to get mad."

"I'm not mad!" Katy yelled. Then she drew in a calming breath. The light changed to green, and Katy eased forward.

"But think about it for a minute, Katy," Shelby said while Katy gritted her teeth and stared ahead. "Like Trish and Cora said, he *is* cute. And I think the reason he acts so obnoxious sometimes is just to get your attention."

Jonathan had told Katy the same thing. She clenched her teeth so hard her jaw ached.

Shelby went on. "When he knocks off all the annoying stuff, he's actually pretty nice."

Katy wished she could plug her ears, but her hands were busy driving.

"He let you borrow his horse and cart, and I heard someone at your church say he's been going in to Schellberg every week to take care of your aunt and uncle's yard and even playing with the boys for a while to keep them occupied." She reached across the seat and tapped Katy's shoulder. "So is it possible you might be able to like him ... someday?"

Katy grunted.

"Not now, necessarily, but maybe later, when he's grown up a little more and stop being such a tease?"

Caleb not teasing? Katy had a hard time imagining it. She turned on the blinker and pulled into the mall parking lot. She found a parking spot as close to the doors as possible for Shelby's sake, then put the car in park. She shut off the motor and lowered her head, toying with the silver key.

"He's really not that bad, Katy." Shelby spoke so softly Katy had a hard time hearing her over the pounding of her own heart. "And dating Caleb wouldn't create any conflict for you with your dad or the church."

"It might with Annika." Katy grasped the most ready excuse. "She likes him, you know."

A sly smile curled Shelby's lips. "I'm not so sure about that. I saw her flirting pretty hard-core with a couple of the guys at her party, and today she kept talking to Todd."

That figures ... Just when Katy needed Annika to save her from Caleb's attention, she had to set her sights on someone else. Katy curled her fist around the key. She couldn't find another reason to argue. "I don't want to talk about it." She forced a smile. "Let's just go eat some ice cream and not think about boys at all, okay?"

Shelby grinned. "Works for me!"

But after Katy bought Caleb's ice cream and he thanked her with a big smile and a light nudge on her elbow, she had a hard time enjoying her own treat. In a lot of ways, Shelby made sense. *But Caleb Penner? I can't think of him that way!... Can I?*

Chapter Thirteen

When they left the mall to return to their cars, Todd pointed overhead. "Wow ... look what rolled in. Those clouds look vicious. We've got a storm coming."

Annika hugged herself and shivered. "I bet it hits before we reach Schellberg."

The others murmured in agreement, and Katy's heart skipped a beat. She'd never driven in a rainstorm. She curled her hand around Shelby's elbow. "We better hurry." She'd want to move Shadow and Saydee into the main barn if the weather got too bad. The lean-to in the pasture provided an adequate shelter, but the horses — especially the baby — might be scared by a big storm.

The three cars carrying kids to Schellberg formed a convoy as they left Salina, with Katy in the last position. She didn't mind being at the back until they turned off the highway onto the dirt roads. Then she had to fight to see past the cloud of dust created by Caleb's and Todd's cars. When dime-sized raindrops began splatting the windshield, the dust stuck in the moisture, further hindering her vision.

She snapped on the windshield wipers and groaned. "Oh, I hate driving in this!"

"Just back off so you don't catch their dust," Shelby advised. "You know the way home—you don't have to stay on their tail."

Katy knew Shelby was right, but the sooner she let Shelby off at the house, the sooner she could take the cart to the pasture and herd Shadow and Saydee in close. But as her visibility worsened, she knew it wasn't safe to drive so close to the others when she couldn't see the road clearly. She'd have to slow down.

As Katy fell back, storm clouds boiled overhead and released rain in a torrent. Raindrops lashed the car, settling the dust, but the onslaught of rain blocked her vision. Frightened by the fierce assault, Katy slowed to a crawl. She clung to the steering wheel so tightly her fingers hurt, and she squinted through the windshield wipers while silently praying for safety. Shelby, normally chatty, fell silent, which allowed Katy to focus on driving.

Both girls heaved a sigh of relief when Katy pulled into her driveway. She drove as close to the back door as possible. The moment she put the car into park, Dad came racing out of the house with an umbrella held over his head.

He popped the passenger door open. "Shelby, I'll get you inside first, then I'll come back for Katy." He didn't bother with her crutches, but just wrapped his arm around her waist and half-carried her into the house. Then he came back out. "C'mon, Katy-girl—let's go."

The raindrops pounding on the car's roof sounded like a band of drums. She hollered over the concert, "I'll come in, but only to put on my rain gear—I need to go check on

Saydee. She's never been in a storm before. I'm afraid she'll be spooked by it."

Dad shook his head. "Don't bother."

"But, Dad!"

"The horses are already in the barn," Dad said. He gestured for her to slide across the seat. "Come on—let's get in."

Katy reached into the backseat and pulled Shelby's crutches with her as she slid to Dad. Together they ran the short distance to the house, their feet splashing muddy water with every step. In the shelter of the little mudroom, Katy kicked off her soggy sandals and tried to brush the excess moisture from her skirt. She grinned at Dad. "We need a bigger umbrella."

"Or a carport on the side of the house to drive under," Dad said. His pant legs were soaked to his knees, the bottom several inches brown and dripping with mud. He removed his boots and grunted in irritation. "I'm going to have to change—I can't stay in these wet clothes."

Katy grimaced. "Sorry you got so wet bringing us in." Then she looked him up and down. "How'd you get Shadow and Saydee in without getting soaked head to toe?"

"I didn't bring them," he said. He ushered Katy into the kitchen and gestured to the table where Shelby, Rosemary, and Jonathan Richter sat together. "Jonathan did."

Katy's eyes landed on Jonathan's smiling face, and she stopped so quickly her bare feet squeaked on the linoleum floor. "Oh ..."

"He saw the storm building when he was out with them," Dad explained, "and he brought them close well before it hit. Then we started visiting, and the storm arrived. I didn't want to send him on until it cleared."

"So you're still here …" *What an idiotic thing to say!* Katy wished she could snatch the words back.

Dad gawked at her in surprise. "Katy …" His voice held admonition.

Katy's ears flamed hot. "I didn't mean — " She gulped. She began inching toward the doorway to the dining room. "I need to go change." Her gaze turned to Shelby. "Do you …?"

Shelby shook her head. "Your dad kept me pretty dry. I'll stay here and sip this wonderful cinnamon tea Mrs. Lambright just poured for me."

Katy gave a quick nod and shot through the dining room to the staircase. She clattered upstairs, her feet making almost as much noise as the crash of thunder that rattled the windows of the house. She changed quickly into a dry dress — her favorite purple-on-purple checks one — and then took the time to pop off her water-speckled headcovering, redo her bun so her hair lay smooth against her head, and put on a fresh cap. She looked in the mirror. One satin ribbon lay rumpled against her shoulder. She smoothed it and gave a satisfied nod.

Presentable.

Drawing in a huge breath, she returned to the kitchen at a much more sedate pace. Dad had already changed into dry work trousers and sat in the fourth chair, but when Katy entered, he bounced up.

"Here you go, Katy-girl. Sit down and join your friends."

Jonathan jumped up too. "Katy can have my seat. I should probably head on back to Dan and Sandra's."

"Nonsense," Rosemary said. "Listen to that thunder! It sounds like it's booming right over our heads. Where

there's thunder, there's lightning, and it isn't safe to be outside. They wouldn't expect you to be out in the storm. Just
stay put." She aimed a crinkling smile at Katy. "I'll pour
Katy a cup of tea, then Samuel and I will leave you young
folks alone to chat."

Jonathan settled back into his chair without an argument, and Rosemary bustled to the stove. On her way past
Katy, she whispered, "Sit. Enjoy." Her eyes twinkled.

Katy felt her ears heating again, but she slid into the
chair Rosemary had vacated. She forced herself to take
slow, shallow breaths to bring her racing pulse under control while Rosemary poured a cup of tea. Her stepmother
placed the cup in front of her, then she and Dad disappeared into the front part of the house.

Shelby pushed the sugar bowl and a spoon across the
table to Katy. "Jonathan was telling me about his work
with horses at his dad's horse farm." She propped her chin
in her hand and gazed at him with longing. "It must be
really fun to spend every day with horses. I love horses —
Katy and I haven't had nearly enough time with Shadow
and Saydee so far. Horses are such beautiful animals.
Majestic, really."

"I enjoy working with them," Jonathan said. He'd finished his cup of tea, and he played with the empty mug,
rolling it between his palms while he spoke. "As you say,
they're majestic animals. So much power, yet they have
a gentle strength. A man learns a great deal of patience,
working with horses. Dad always says training horses is
good practice for living life wisely."

Katy took a cautious sip of her tea. The sweet cinnamon
flavor tingled on her tongue. Outside, the wind calmed,

turning the raucous pounding of drops against the roof and windows into a gentle patter. She began to relax. "So do you think you'll raise horses for a living too?"

Jonathan chuckled. "Well, as I was telling your dad earlier, I'm the youngest of six boys. So I have plenty of competition for taking over my dad's business. My two oldest brothers have already gone into other occupations. Joshua works with his wife's father on their farm, and Judah opened a farming implement business near Bird-in-Hand. Then Jeremiah and Jerrod—they're the twins—opened a wagon-building and harness-making shop on the edge of my dad's property. My other brother, Jerome, works full-time with my dad and uncle. He'll probably be the one to take over the horse ranch when Dad decides to quit."

Katy, listening, tried to imagine growing up in such a large family. The picture wouldn't gel. She said, "So what about you? What do you want to do?"

Jonathan lowered his chin, and his forehead creased into a series of frown lines. "I'll probably end up working in Jeremiah and Jerrod's shop. They said they could use me, and I know my dad would approve."

Katy caught the hint of melancholy in his tone. She leaned forward. "I didn't ask what your dad wants you to do. I asked what you want to do."

His head lifted, and his gaze smacked into hers. For several seconds he didn't reply, and Katy wondered if she'd insulted him. But she didn't retract her question. She really wanted to know. She wanted to know everything about him.

Finally he drew in a big breath. "What I want to do I can't do, so there's no sense in even thinking about it."

Shelby set her empty cup aside and released a little
snort. "You can't say something like that and just leave us
hanging. Come on — 'fess up. We won't tell anybody. What
do you want to do?" Her grin turned teasing. "Do you
wanna be, like, the first Mennonite to fly in a space shuttle
to the moon?"

Katy swallowed a giggle, imagining Jonathan with his
flat-brimmed church hat atop the globelike headgear of an
astronaut's suit.

"No, not that." Jonathan laughed lightly too, but then
he shrugged. "But you're not far from what I want."

Shelby's eyes flew wide. "Really?"

Jonathan nodded, his face sad. "Really. I love science.
Especially space science. Our galaxy is so amazing —
God's creation ... I never tire of looking at the stars. I'd
love to study what all is out there." His expression turned
pensive. "If I could, I'd go to college and try to become
some kind of astronomer. Or a meteorologist — that would
be okay too. Or even a high school teacher so I could share
what I love with others." He sighed, turning to face Katy.
"That's why I'm a little jealous of you, Katy. Getting to go
to high school and earn your diploma." He angled his head
to the side, the pose very boyish and appealing. "What do
you plan to do after you graduate?"

The question pierced Katy. Would she get to graduate?
She wasn't even sure she'd go on to her junior year. So
much depended on Aunt Rebecca's treatments and recov-
ery. She answered carefully. "I'm like you — I'd like to go
to college, if Dad and the elders allow it. That's why I want
to train Saydee to pull a buggy — she'll fetch a better price,
and I'll need the money for college." She risked sharing her

dream with this visiting boy who gazed at her with open interest on his handsome face. "I want to be a journalist."

"Really?" Jonathan's face lit. "For newspapers or magazines?"

Katy shrugged. She sipped the cooling tea. "Either, I guess. I haven't really decided. I just know I love to write."

"She's good at it too," Shelby contributed. "You should read her poems."

Katy sent Shelby a frantic look. Her poetry was private, revealing some of her deepest feelings. She'd never share any of those with a boy!

"And," Shelby went on, "she wrote this amazing oration for forensics competition that wowed the judges. Maybe she'll show you her medals sometime."

Jonathan said, "I'd like to see them."

But Katy knew she'd never show Jonathan the medals she won at contests. Showing them would be the same as bragging. She didn't want Jonathan to think of her as prideful. She ducked her head and pretended great interest in the remaining contents of her mug.

Jonathan chuckled. "But maybe I better not see them. They'd only make me more jealous."

Katy sneaked a peek at him and saw his lips twitch in a self-conscious grin. A giggle found its way from her throat. He didn't claim to be perfect. She liked that.

Suddenly Jonathan jerked, seeming to examine the ceiling. Katy, uncertain, looked upward too. At the same time, they lowered their heads and looked across the table at each other.

Jonathan said, "The rain stopped."

At the same time, Katy said, "It's quiet."

Shelby snickered. "Great minds think alike."

Jonathan's cheeks blotched pink while Katy's ears heated.

He pushed his chair back. "Since the storm's passed, I should go."

Katy stood too. "I—I enjoyed ... visiting."

He smiled—a funny, almost crooked smile that made Katy feel like her insides were melting. "Me too. But I need to ..."

"Yes, it's probably time for you to ..." Couldn't either of them finish a sentence?

Shelby lurched upright and reached for her crutches. "Let's walk him out, Katy."

Katy gave herself a little nudge and gestured toward the dining room doorway rather than escorting him to the mudroom back door. She was certain his cousin's truck waited in front. She and Shelby followed him to the front room, where he stopped and thanked Dad and Rosemary for their hospitality. His manners pleased Katy, and she could tell by the expressions on her parents' faces that they appreciated his polite ways too.

He opened the door and turned back. "'Bye, Katy and Shelby." Then he fixed his gaze on Katy. "You ..." He licked his lips, flicking a quick glance at her dad. "You don't work on Monday, right?"

Katy's hands began to tremble. She clasped them behind her back. "Well, yes and no. The fabric shop's always closed on Monday. But I left before I finished the cleanup chores today. So I'll probably go in and run the vacuum cleaner and dust the shelves and so forth—get the place looking nice for Tuesday."

"With today's heavy rain, and the storm they're predicting for tomorrow, the fields will probably be too wet for Dan and me to do much on Monday. Could I, um, maybe pick you up — and Shelby too, of course — and ... well, take you into the café for lunch?" The pink streaks in his cheeks deepened to a blazing red. "I'd like to talk to you a little more. About school and ..." Again, he glanced at her dad. "Something else."

Katy looked at Dad. "Would it be okay, Dad?"

Dad turned to Rosemary. He'd started seeking her approval when granting or denying Katy's requests. Rosemary didn't say anything, but she smiled. Dad gave a barely discernible nod, as if the two of them had communicated silently.

Dad faced Jonathan and Katy. "I think that would be fine. Maybe Katy could stay in town after lunch to do her cleaning, and one of us could pick her up later in the afternoon."

Their plans seemed set. Jonathan grinned. "Good. I'll come by around ... eleven thirty?"

"That would be perfect," Katy said.

"All right then. See you Monday, Katy." He slipped out the door.

Katy closed it slowly, peeking through the narrowing crack at his retreating form. What did he mean when he said he wanted to talk to her about "something else"? The curiosity might drive her crazy.

She clicked the door closed and turned to find both Dad and Rosemary grinning at her. She put her hands on her hips. "What?"

"Oh, nothing," Dad said innocently.

From the backyard, the sound of a car horn blared. Dad leaped up. "Must be Caleb, wondering where I am. It's milking time." He paused to drop a kiss on Rosemary's cheek before charging through the house.

Katy stood as still as if her feet had sent down roots. Her conversation with Shelby about Caleb and remembrances of her time visiting with Jonathan bounced around in her brain, raising a variety of confusing emotions.

Rosemary cleared her throat, and Katy looked at her. Rosemary's smile grew tender. "He's a nice boy, Katy."

She didn't indicate which boy, and Katy realized the comment could apply to either Jonathan or Caleb at that moment. Katy's stomach twisted into a tight knot. She swallowed. "Yes, I know." *But which boy is the right one for me?*

Chapter Fourteen

"I'd like a BLT, french fries, and a Coke, please," Katy told Yvonne. Both Shelby and Jonathan had ordered cheese-burgers, fries, and milkshakes, and Katy had been tempted to do the same. But she didn't want Jonathan to think she was copying him. Besides, she loved the café's bacon, lettuce, and tomato sandwich on their home-baked wheat bread with lots of mayonnaise.

"Coming right up." Yvonne whirled and returned to the kitchen with her skirts swishing around her knees. She'd been a lot friendlier with Jonathan in the booth than she'd been with Katy and Shelby the day they'd come in alone. But Katy decided not to mention that fact.

Shelby looked around the busy café. She leaned close to Katy and whispered, "I can't believe how many people are in here. And lots of them are non-Mennonite."

Katy swallowed a chuckle. It was easy to differentiate between the Schellberg residents and the visiting patrons. Their clothing gave them away. "I know. That's pretty typical, actually. People from neighboring communities come over here to eat because they enjoy the home cooking."

Shelby continued to survey the other customers, and Katy looked across the booth to Jonathan. She felt that telltale heat creep into her ears when she realized he was staring at her. His fervent expression made her feel weak and quivery inside. She'd never understand the effect this boy had on her.

"You said you wanted to talk to me about ... something," she reminded him.

He gave a little jolt, as if awakening from a dream, and propped his elbows on the edge of the table. "Yes, I do. Two things, actually." His change in demeanor—from deeply seeking to businesslike—helped put Katy at ease. "First of all, school. What did you do to convince the elders to let you go?"

Katy cringed, remembering the agonizing weeks before she gathered the courage to ask Dad if she could seek permission from the council. "First of all, I prayed. A *lot.* I wanted to make sure it was something I was even supposed to pursue. I knew I couldn't be happy following my dream if my dream wasn't what God wanted for me."

He nodded, his brow furrowed in a serious frown. "That's always best."

"Then I talked to my dad, and he set up a meeting with the elders to discuss the possibility." She sighed as she thought about the long meeting and the numerous questions she'd fielded. "Since no one in Schellberg had ever wanted to go beyond ninth grade, the elders had a lot of concerns. Mostly that what I wanted was really best for me, and also that my going wouldn't create a rift in the community with the other young people. The council didn't want the others to feel as though I got an unfair advantage or something."

Shelby looked at Katy with sympathy. "You sure stepped out on a limb. And I can think of a few people who tried to saw it off behind you."

Katy chuckled at Shelby's picturesque speech. "That's a good way to put it." She turned to Jonathan again. "The first months were pretty uncomfortable all the way around—for me at the high school because I ... well, I stuck out." She shrugged. "It was uncomfortable for me here in town too, because some fellowship members really didn't approve of the decision to let me go. But I think people have settled in with it now for the most part."

Yvonne scurried over and delivered their drinks. "Food's coming—Dad's still gotta fry the bacon, then it'll be out." She took off again.

Katy watched Yvonne go. She shrugged. "There will always be some who watch me, waiting to see if I'm picking up worldly habits." Aunt Rebecca had been one of the worst ones, but since her illness she'd been less disapproving. Others who'd been uncertain seemed to follow her aunt's example and relax too. "But knowing they're watching probably isn't such a bad thing. It makes me accountable to stay true to my convictions."

She inwardly cringed, recalling how close she'd come to bending her convictions when she'd been chosen as homecoming attendant. "I don't do everything right," she felt obliged to admit, "but I do my best. And I try to learn from my mistakes."

"That's all any of us can do," Jonathan said in a musing tone. "And have the kids at the high school been okay with you being there? Obviously, some of them are okay with it, or Shelby and you wouldn't be such good friends, right?"

Katy and Shelby exchanged a look and they both giggled. Katy could tell Jonathan lots of stories about how she was treated and how awful it felt to be the "weird little Amish girl" on campus. In the end, she said, "I'll always stick out — I can't help it. But the ones who matter most accept me being there. That's all that matters."

"That makes sense." Jonathan unwrapped a straw and jammed it into his milkshake. But then, instead of taking a drink, he leaned forward a little more and lowered his voice, as if unwilling to let any other patrons overhear him. "To be honest, the reason my dad sent me to spend the summer working for Dan was to give me time to 'come to my senses.' Maybe he even hoped I'd find out I liked harvesting corn and would set my sights on farming instead of stargazing."

He turned to the window, and it seemed to Katy he drank in the view of the sky over the roofs of the buildings across the street. Then he looked at her again. "But he didn't figure on me meeting a girl who was spunky enough to ask permission to attend public high school and then actually follow through with it." His smile warmed Katy from her head to her toes. "Now that I know your fellowship allowed you to go to public school, it's inspired me, Katy. I — " He swallowed, his Adam's apple visibly bobbing above the buttoned neck of his shirt. "I intend to ask to go on to high school too."

Shelby released a little squeal. Several people turned and looked in their direction, and she clamped her hand over her mouth for a moment. She shot an apologetic look at the other diners then reached across the table and squeezed Jonathan's wrist. "That's fantastic! Follow your dreams, Jonathan. There's, like, this saying." She scrunched her face, thinking. Her expression brightened. "Oh, yeah! 'Aim for the moon; even if you miss, you'll land among the stars.'"

Jonathan smiled. "I like that. I'll have to write it down and remember it." He shifted his attention to Katy. "So what do you think?"

Katy didn't know what to say. She'd never imagined inspiring someone else to seek further education. The idea both thrilled and humbled her. Before she found words, Yvonne bustled over, balancing their plates on her arm. She slid their plates in front of them, removed a bottle of ketchup from her apron pocket and plopped it on the table, then asked, "Anything else?"

"Looks fine," Jonathan answered for all of them.

"Holler if you need something later." Yvonne shot off again.

Jonathan's eyes moved quickly between Shelby and Katy. "So ..." He looked bashful all of a sudden. "Do you wanna pray on your own, or would you like me to ...?"

"Go ahead," Shelby said.

Jonathan bowed his head and offered a blessing for their meal. Even though it was short, he didn't stammer over his words, and Katy believed it was sincere. Shelby and Jonathan immediately began eating, but Katy sat for a few moments, absorbing the significance of what had just happened. Although she'd seen Bryce and even Caleb bow their heads over their plates, she'd never heard them pray aloud. Seeing Jonathan willing to pray in a public place —

even though it was just a short prayer of blessing—drew her to him. She admired him. And admiration went deeper than infatuation, she realized.

"Katy, you want ketchup for your fries?"

Shelby's voice jerked Katy from her inner reflections. She nodded and took the bottle. By the time she'd lifted the first french fry to her lips, she'd set aside her wonder and was able to act normally again.

Midway through eating, Shelby said, "Jonathan, you said you wanted to talk to Katy about two things. You already talked about school. What's the other thing?"

Katy wished Shelby hadn't asked. She'd gotten the impression on Saturday that the second topic would be very serious. She'd lain awake far into the night, thinking about his expression and his solemn tone. All kinds of thoughts had tumbled through her brain, and she'd finally gotten out of bed and recorded all of it in her journal so she could set her anxiety aside. But now the various emotions rolled over her again, thanks to Shelby's question.

"He's eating—he doesn't have to talk now," she said, hoping Jonathan might let the second topic die. After all, if he intended to ask if he could begin pursuing her as a potential beau, she'd have to say no. And she didn't know if she'd have the strength to do it. He was becoming more appealing by the minute.

Jonathan shook his head. "It's okay. I'm glad Shelby said something so I didn't forget." He held a fry between his finger and thumb and used it to point at Katy. "It has to do with your desire to be a journalist."

Katy nearly wilted. But from relief or disappointment?

She gave herself a mental kick and forced herself to focus on Jonathan's next words.

"I don't know if you get the newspaper, but there's an Amish woman from Quarryville who writes a daily column that's printed in newspapers all over the United States." His eyes shone with excitement. "She writes it by lantern light, in longhand at her kitchen table, and people are fascinated because it gives them a glimpse into the life of an Amish family."

Jonathan quickly stuck the french fry in his mouth, chewed, and swallowed. "I was thinking ... maybe you could do the same thing. Write articles for the paper in Salina about what it's like to live on a dairy farm, where you don't have a telephone or television, and you have to do chores by hand instead of with machines like other kids have." He picked up his burger, but instead of taking a bite, he sat looking at Katy over the top of the half-eaten sandwich. "I bet people would find it interesting, and it'd give you a chance to practice doing what you want to do — be a journalist."

Katy stared at Jonathan, openmouthed. She'd never considered becoming a journalist without having a college degree. But surely that Amish woman didn't have a college degree, and yet she was published. Nationally published, according to Jonathan. Her heart pounded in excitement. "Do you really think I could do it?"

Shelby let out a hoot of laughter. "*Think?* Girlfriend, I *know* you could do it! You're an awesome writer. I bet if you went into the office of the *Salina Gazette* and gave them some writing samples, they'd hire you on the spot."

Katy giggled self-consciously. She appreciated Shelby's confidence, but she wondered if her friend was being completely realistic. A person didn't get a writing job by just walking in and asking for it. Or did she? "I'd have to ask Dad," she said slowly.

Shelby grabbed her arm. "But you'll do it? You'll try?"

Katy sucked in her breath and held it. She looked from Shelby's hopeful face to Jonathan's. She let out her air on a self-conscious giggle. "Yes. I'll try."

"Awesome!" Shelby punched the air, earning another round of curious glances. But she didn't act embarrassed this time. She snatched up her cheeseburger. "Oh, wow, Katy, I can't wait 'til you talk to your dad. And I want to go with you when you go to the newspaper office so I can watch you win them over." She chomped down on her burger then spoke around the bite. "Jonathan, that idea is beyond epic. I never would've thought of it. I am *so* glad you came to Schellberg."

Katy nibbled at her sandwich, her heart thudding wildly in her chest. *Is this why he came to Schellberg? Not to be my boyfriend, but to send me on the path to the writing career God has picked for me?*

Chapter Fifteen

"Everything's balanced to the penny. *Finally.*"

Katy turned from straightening the last row of cloth bolts and grinned at Shelby. Making the cash in the register drawer match with the books had taken the better part of Saturday morning. Of course, part of the delay was from taking care of a steady stream of customers. The fabric shop had always gotten its share of business, but it seemed since Aunt Rebecca's illness people had made an even greater effort to purchase fabric and notions. Katy saw it as the community's way of supporting her aunt, and she appreciated it. But the busy days also exhausted her.

She balled her fist on her hip and pretended to scold her friend. "Well, now that it's done, instead of sounding disgusted, you ought to be delighted."

"I'll save my delight for when we visit the newspaper office and find out you're going to be the next freelance columnist for the *Salina Gazette*," Shelby said.

Katy closed her eyes for a moment and allowed herself to imagine the newspaper editor giving an enthusiastic yes to her request. Since she and Shelby worked at the fabric store every day during the week, they hadn't been able to drive to Salina yet, but — using Shelby's cell phone — they'd done plenty in preparation.

Katy's debate and forensic coach from Salina High North, Mr. Gorsky, agreed to give her a recommendation; the editor scheduled a meeting with Katy on the coming Monday morning; and she and Shelby sorted through all of Katy's essays from English class and her poetry journal for the best samples of her writing. And she'd prayed. She'd prayed with Dad and Rosemary, with Shelby, and in private more times than she could count.

She bowed her head and released another heartfelt petition. *If this is Your will for me, open wide the door, God.*

"You know," Shelby said, intruding upon Katy's thoughts, "it's too bad we have to drive on highways to get to Salina. Wouldn't it be cool to take the horse and cart? They could photograph you on the buggy and use that as your signature pic." She giggled, her eyes crinkling with humor. "That'd sure capture attention!"

Katy groaned. "Oh, no ..."

Shelby laughed. "'Course, your little ribboned cap ought to be enough ... so we can just go in the car, like we'd already planned."

"As if I'd change those plans!" Katy shook her head, picturing Shelby and her rolling down the highway in Caleb's two-wheeled cart with Rocky pulling them. She sighed. "I just hope my writing is good enough."

"Your writing's more than good enough," Shelby said, warming Katy with her loyalty. "It'll come down to whether they have the column space. But if they like the idea enough, they can make space."

Katy wondered if "making space" meant booting some other writer. She hoped not. She didn't think she would be able to enjoy having her own weekly column if it meant someone else had lost their spot on the paper. She adjusted the final bolt and turned from the shelves. "Well, I think we're done here. Want to grab some lunch at the café or just head to the house?"

Shelby tapped her lips. "How about if we ask for sandwiches to go and take the cart to the pasture? I haven't seen Saydee in two weeks." She jolted, her eyes flying wide. "Katy, do you realize I've been here almost a whole month? My folks'll be back in two weeks, and two weeks after that school will start again. This summer sure is flying by."

Katy thought about all the plans she and Shelby had made for their time together — calligraphy and quilting projects, lots of time with Saydee and Shadow ... But instead they'd spent their weeks running the fabric shop. And it didn't look as if things would change. Aunt Rebecca wasn't handling the chemotherapy treatments well at all. She could hardly lift her head from the pillow and had lost so much weight she looked like a skeleton.

The doctors had tried several different medicines to bring the nausea, tiredness, and muscle aches under control, but nothing seemed to help. Katy bit down on her lower lip, sympathy for her aunt rising alongside a selfish worry that constantly nibbled at her mind. Even if Aunt Rebecca's chemo treatments ended tomorrow, when would she have the strength to take over the shop again? Katy was glad to help Aunt Rebecca, but she couldn't help wishing she and Shelby would have been able to have a bit more free time. And she couldn't help wondering about school.

But at least for now they could have some fun. "Sure, we can do that," Katy said. "Let me put the vacuum cleaner away, and then we'll go next door."

Twenty minutes later Katy and Shelby climbed into the cart and headed for the pasture. They munched ham and cheese sandwiches, pickles, and potato chips while they rode beneath a clear blue sky. Hot wind dried the bread on the sandwiches and chased a few chips over the edge of the cart, but Katy didn't mind. Being outside in the sun, with the breeze tossing Shelby's hair and making Katy's ribbons dance, left her feeling young and carefree. She savored the minutes.

They turned the corner leading to the pasture, and Shelby poked Katy on the shoulder. She pointed. "Is that the Richter's truck?"

Katy squinted. "It sure looks like it." Immediately, her palms began to sweat and her pulse tripped into a speedier beat. "Jonathan must be with the horses again."

"I wish we'd known he'd be out here. We could've brought him a sandwich," Shelby said.

Katy drew Rocky to a halt at the pickup's tailgate and hopped down. She helped Shelby out and then they moved to the fence. Jonathan spotted them and walked in from the pasture. Saydee pranced along beside him, with Shadow close on Jonathan's heels like a pair of overgrown dogs. Katy couldn't help but smile at the sight.

When they reached the fence, Shelby stretched her hand over the top line of barbed wire and cupped Saydee's jaw. The colt nickered but didn't pull away. Shelby laughed, running both hands over Saydee's head and neck. "Wow! Look at this, Katy—she's letting me touch her!"

Katy watched, amazed and grateful. Jonathan's time with the horses had created a tremendous change in the foal. She beamed at him. "You must've worked with her a lot."

Jonathan shrugged. "Oh, not so much—just for a few minutes on my lunch hour and a little more time in the evenings. It's not so hard to get a horse to trust you if you start when they're as young as Saydee." He moved to the gate and let himself out. He ambled to Shelby's side and reached across the top wire on the fence to give the colt's ears a scratch. "I've gotten pretty attached to both Shadow and Saydee. Thanks for letting me hang around."

Shadow nosed Katy's shoulder, and Katy laughed. She rubbed Shadow's nose while she spoke to Jonathan. "Thank you for coming out. They've been pretty much neglected this summer, I'm afraid. I'm glad somebody could spend time with them. And ..." She hadn't talked to Jonathan since last Monday when he'd taken Shelby and her to lunch and planted the idea of writing a column about her Mennonite lifestyle. "Thanks too for telling me about that Amish woman. I have an interview with the special feature editor of the *Salina Gazette* on Monday to talk about the possibility of writing for the paper."

Jonathan's face broke into a huge smile. He snatched off his bill cap, punched the air with it, then slapped it back into place. "That's great, Katy! What time is your interview?"

She crinkled her brow. Did he want to come along too? "Why?"

"So I can be praying about it," he said. "I'll stop what I'm doing and pray while you're in the interview, if you'd like. For God's favor for you."

Tears pricked behind Katy's nose. Dad and Rosemary had promised to do the same thing, but she wouldn't have expected Jonathan—someone she'd only met and hardly knew at all—to stop and pray for her. She blurted, "Why do you care so much?"

His face blotched with pink, and he looked down while scuffing his boot in the dry grass. "You hope to be a journalist. *'Hope deferred maketh the heart sick,'*" he quoted. A funny little grin twitched his lips. "A girl as pretty as you should never be heartsick."

He thinks I'm pretty! Heat rushed to Katy's face. She stared at the ground, willing her galloping heart to return to normal. "Th-thanks, Jonathan."

"So ..." He waited until she peeked at him. "What time is that interview?"

Katy giggled. She couldn't help it. The happiness inside had to spill out. "Ten o'clock."

He adjusted the brim of his hat, smiling at her. "Ten o'clock. I'll be praying—you can count on it. But now ..." He slipped his hands into his pockets and inched sideways, moving toward the pickup truck. "I need to get back to work before Dan sends out a search party. See you, Katy ... Shelby."

Shelby waved and went back to stroking Saydee. "'Bye!"

Katy took two steps toward Jonathan and held out her hand. "Wait!" He paused with the door open and one foot inside the cab. Katy dashed to his side. Breathless, she made a promise. "I'll be praying for you too—to be able to follow your dream. You—you shouldn't have a sick heart, either."

He didn't say anything, but he didn't need to. His smile was all the response Katy needed.

✣

Sunday's worship ended with a special time of prayer for Aunt Rebecca, this time for her strength to persevere. Kneeling next to Lori and Lola, Katy experienced the desire to wrap her arms around her cousins and offer them comfort. If it was hard for her to see Aunt Rebecca suffer, it must be excruciating for the twins to witness the changes in their mother.

When the elders ended the service, Katy handed Shelby her crutches and they met up with Annika on the lawn. Annika gave Katy a quick hug and said, "I can't believe how little I've seen you this summer. Do you think maybe you and Shelby could bring the cart over this afternoon? We could work on calligraphy letters or just hang out in the barn and talk."

"I'll check with Dad," Katy said, "but it sounds good to me. I doubt Gramma Ruthie will be able to help Shelby with that quilting project like we'd planned. She's so busy with Uncle Albert and Aunt Rebecca's boys."

Annika touched Katy's arm. "Your aunt's cancer has changed a lot of things, hasn't it?"

Katy didn't want to think about everything that had changed since cancer intruded in her family. Instead of answering Annika's question, she said, "Let me go ask Dad about visiting you this afternoon. Stay here, Shelby—I'll be right back."

She left Shelby and Annika to chat and jogged toward Dad. He stood in the shade beside the church building, talking with two of the elders. Rather than interrupt their conversation, she hung back. She couldn't make out what the other men were saying, but she heard Dad's low-toned reply: "Let's not jump to conclusions. It could just be a rumor."

The others murmured something in reply and then ambled off. Katy moved to Dad's side and touched his arm. He jumped as if she'd startled him. She frowned. "Are you all right?"

"I'm fine." His smile seemed forced, though. He slipped his arm across her shoulders and aimed her toward the middle of the yard. "What did you need?"

Katy repeated Annika's request then asked, "Would that be all right?"

"So you aren't planning to eat with Annika — just visit her later?"

"Yes."

Dad offered a quick nod. "That would be fine. Rosemary and I will probably go into Schellberg this afternoon to check on Rebecca. We might not be back in time to fix supper or do the milking. Would you . . . ?"

Katy refrained from releasing a sigh. She'd hoped for a free afternoon, but how could she refuse to help? "That's fine, Dad. We'll make sure we're back by five so I can help with the milking if I'm needed, and Shelby and I can put something on the table for supper."

"It'll probably just be setting out leftovers," Dad said, "so it shouldn't tax you too much." He paused and stared across the yard at something, his brows pulled down in confusion. Or worry.

Katy bumped her arm against his side. "Dad, are you sure you're all right?"

"Hmm?" He gave another little jerk and shifted to smile down at her. "Yes, yes, just fine. Don't worry. Why don't you and Shelby go to the car now. I'll get Rosemary and we'll head home."

Katy moved slowly to obey, a troublesome thought plaguing her. Something was bothering Dad—something he didn't want her to know. A second thought intruded: if anyone would be aware of something amiss in Schellberg, it would be Annika. Somehow that girl managed to gather every bit of information from every source available. And Katy would have her cornered for the afternoon.

Katy hurried to her friends, determination squaring her jaw. She didn't like to encourage gossip, but she'd pry whatever she could from Annika when she had the chance.

Chapter Sixteen

Annika's little brothers wanted to play in the barn, and it was too hot to be in Annika's second-story bedroom, so the girls crowded into the two-wheeled cart's seat and drove to the pond behind Katy's house. They spread out an old blanket Annika had dragged along and sat in the shade of a straggly cottonwood tree.

Shelby leaned against the tree's trunk with one knee bent and her cast-wrapped foot stretched out. Katy sat cross-legged next to Shelby, and Annika kicked off her shoes and then lay on her stomach. She twirled a dried piece of grass while bouncing her crossed ankles. Since she hadn't talked to Katy much during the summer weeks, she had a lot to say. Shelby and Katy mostly listened, but Katy didn't mind. She relaxed more and more as the minutes slipped away. Even though it was hot, it was bearable in the shade with a nice breeze blowing, and she encouraged Annika to tell them everything the youth of Schellberg had done while she and Shelby had been busy at the fabric shop.

When Annika finally seemed to run out of words, Katy cleared her throat. She plucked a length of grass and stuck it in the corner of her mouth before asking, "Annika, is there anything ... important ... or disconcerting ... stirring in the fellowship?"

Annika scrunched her forehead. "Disconcerting? What's that?"

Shelby answered. "Something that bothers you."

"Oh." Annika didn't seem disconcerted that both Shelby and Katy knew a word she didn't. She scratched her chin. "No, nothing I can think of." Then she pushed up on her elbows and sent a bright look in Katy's direction. "But what do you think of Caleb wanting to go to high school?"

Katy nearly choked on the piece of grass. She flung it aside. "What?"

Annika frowned. "You didn't know? He's at your house every day, so I figured — "

"He's in the *barn* every day," Katy said, "not in the house. And since I've been closing the shop in the late afternoon, I usually don't even get back until he's gone." But why hadn't Dad told her? Or why hadn't Caleb tried to seek her out and discuss something so important with her? Now that he didn't try to pester her all the time, she didn't mind talking with him. She could answer his questions and give him advice. For reasons she couldn't understand, it hurt to be left out of such substantial news.

"Well ..." Annika rolled to a seated position. "He hasn't said anything to me either, but Mom and Dad were talking about it. The elders are considering his request — I mean, they kind of have to after letting you go — but they're half-afraid ..." She hunched her shoulders and giggled.

"What?" Katy and Shelby said at the same time.

Annika smirked at Shelby. "They think maybe Caleb only wants to go because Katy's going." She shifted to look at Katy. "Would it be so surprising that he wants to be with you?"

Katy searched Annika's face for signs of jealousy. But Annika only seemed amused. Katy asked, "And what do you think?"

Annika shrugged again and began breaking the piece of grass into small pieces. "I wouldn't be surprised. Caleb Penner ... interested in *school*?" She snorted. "And after all, he's liked you for a long time." She looked up at the waving tree branches overhead and sighed. "I think he liked me for a little bit, but it didn't last. I figured he'd go after you again. Old habits die hard."

Shelby said, "And that's okay with you?"

Annika made a face. "Well, it wouldn't be except ..." She giggled again. "Todd's started coming around. He's older — eighteen already. And taller. And I love his black hair. I got a peek at our reflection together in the big window of the grocery store, and we just look like we, you know, fit together. Plus he likes me — he really likes *me*. With Caleb, I'd always wonder if I was his second choice." She grinned and flipped her hand in a dismissive gesture. "So Katy's welcome to Caleb."

Katy didn't care for being handed Annika's cast-offs, but she didn't say so.

Shelby sagged against the tree trunk. "Wow ... Caleb Penner asking to go to school. So there might be *two* Mennonite kids at Salina High North next year." She poked Katy with her elbow. "How about that, Katy? You won't be alone."

Katy offered a weak smile and a nod. Shelby and Annika went on talking, but she turned her focus inward. What would it be like, having Caleb at school with her? They wouldn't be in many classes together, since he'd be a sophomore and she was ready for her junior year. But maybe they would ride in together in Caleb's car—no more bus with all those younger, rowdy kids. Instead, she'd start and end her day with Caleb. The thought wasn't as offensive as it once might have been.

Caleb had done some changing lately, Katy mused. He was less obnoxious. More giving. Oh, he still had his moments—he was Caleb, after all. But if he kept making changes, he could end up being pretty decent. Maybe it wouldn't be so bad after all to have more time with him. She liked his family; her family liked him. They shared the same faith. They both wanted to remain in the same community. There were lots of reasons to spend time with Caleb, when she really thought about it.

"Katy?"

Katy jolted and looked at Shelby.

"Did you hear what Annika just said?"

Embarrassed, Katy shook her head.

Shelby laughed. "She asked if you wanted to go back to her place for some lemonade before we go home."

Katy pushed to her feet. "Sounds good to me." She gave Shelby's hands a tug to help her stand, and the girls clambered into the cart. They giggled at the snug fit while rolling toward Annika's house. After their lemonade, Katy helped Shelby back into the cart and then climbed up beside her.

Annika stood in the yard and smiled up at them. "I

hope your interview tomorrow goes well, Katy," she said. "Come by here on your way home and tell me all about it. If you get the job, I'll bake a special cake to celebrate, okay?"

"Thanks—I'd like that," Katy said. She flicked the reins and set Rocky into motion.

"That was nice of her, wanting to bake you a cake," Shelby said.

Katy nodded. It was nice. She and Annika had done some fussing in the past year as they adjusted to growing up, but deep down, they were still good friends. Annika's willingness to celebrate with Katy proved it. *But if I get the job, seeing my name in the newspaper will be celebration enough.*

❖

"Well, Miss Lambright, it's apparent you have some natural ability as a writer."

Katy sat in a chair across from the editor's messy desk and clutched her hands in her lap to keep from nibbling her nails. The editor, Mr. Matthews, didn't smile, but neither did he frown. In fact, he hadn't changed expression once during the thirty minutes he'd spent interviewing her. Katy wasn't able to discern what he was thinking. She wished she could get at least a small clue. She had no idea how to respond to him.

He ran his hand down his thick, gray beard, as if smoothing it. Since he had no hair on his head, Katy presumed the beard gave him something to comb. "According to your English teacher, a Mr."—he leaned sideways and peeked at a paper on the corner of the desktop—"Gorsky, you are dependable and hardworking. Those are admirable qualities."

Katy squeaked, "Thank you, sir."

He nodded. Brusquely. No smile. "Your lack of experience, however, gives me pause."

Katy's heart sank. He was going to send her away.

"The idea is sound, and I do believe there would be at least a modicum of interest in what you've proposed to write. Especially in these frantic times, people yearn for a slower pace — a gentler time." Mr. Matthews leaned back in his chair and fixed Katy with a serious look. "Your articles might provide that."

Katy stifled a laugh. If the man had any idea of her life right now, he wouldn't use the words "a slower pace." She sat quietly and allowed him to continue.

"But to be honest with you, Miss Lambright, I don't believe I could make space in the *Gazette* for something experimental by an unknown writer."

Katy's shoulders sagged. She nodded. "I understand. Thank you for your time." Eager to flee the building and give vent to her disappointment, she rose.

"Now wait a minute." The man waved his hand at her, gesturing for her to sit.

She sank into the chair. Blinking rapidly, she inwardly prayed she wouldn't dissolve into tears and embarrass herself.

"I can't put you in the *Gazette*, but we have a secondary publication — the *Free Bee*. Have you heard of it?"

"Um ... yes, sir." Katy had seen it — someone threw it at the end of the driveway a few times each month. But Dad never brought it to the house to read, he just tossed it into the burn barrel. She held her breath, hoping Mr. Matthews wouldn't ask if she'd read it.

"Then you know it's a smaller paper, delivered once a week free of charge to every resident of Saline County — hence the word 'free' in the title." Mr. Matthews grimaced, as if apologizing. "It's mostly advertisements and notice of items for sale with a few general interest articles. But I wonder if your writing wouldn't work well for its format."

Katy's held breath escaped. She dared to let hope blossom again.

"I wouldn't be able to pay you much — twenty dollars a week — but we can give it a trial run and see what kind of interest it brings." For the first time, the hint of a smile appeared on the corners of the man's lips. "That is, if you're interested."

Katy beamed. "I'm interested!"

"All right then. Come with me." Mr. Matthews rose and rounded the corner of the desk. He ushered Katy into the main room, where partitions separated the various working stations. He guided Katy to a cubicle in the far corner and poked his head around a bright orange partition. "Marge?"

A middle-aged woman with a white-blonde ponytail and green, bejeweled square-framed glasses on the end of her nose looked up from her computer keyboard. "Uh-huh?" She gave Katy a quick perusal from head to toe and up again. Katy tried not to fidget beneath the woman's curious examination.

"This is Kathleen Lambright."

Marge's lips quirked into an impersonal but not unkind smile. "Hello, Kathleen."

"Hello," Katy said in reply. She wished she knew the woman's last name so she could address her properly.

Mr. Matthews said, "She's going to start writing a weekly article for the *Free Bee*. She'll need to complete the standard paperwork for employment, and I assume" — he raised his eyebrows and peered at Katy — "she will *not* be submitting via email attachment."

Katy nodded rapidly, her ribbons bouncing against her shoulders. "That's correct. I don't own a computer."

Marge pulled several pieces of paper from a gray file drawer. "Do you have Internet on a cell phone?"

"We don't have any phones at home," Katy said.

"You could fax us your article from the library," Mr. Matthews suggested.

Katy cringed. "We don't have a library in Schellberg." She was making things difficult for them. Would they change their minds?

Mr. Matthews stroked his beard again. "Hmm, communicating with this young lady may prove challenging." He looked at Katy. "You'll need to be sure your article is on the editor's desk a week prior to publication." He shifted his focus back to Marge. "Give her a publishing schedule. Also put together a supply of envelopes and a sheet of mailing labels so she'll be set to submit with good ol' snail mail. Talk to Doug in typesetting about transcribing her articles for us."

Marge opened a little cabinet behind her. "Will do."

Mr. Matthews stuck out his hand, and Katy shook it. "Welcome aboard, Miss Lambright. And best of luck to you."

Chapter Seventeen

"I need to tell Annika and Dad and Rosemary and Gramma Ruthie and Grampa Ben and Mr. Gorsky and — " Katy gasped. She was running out of air. She giggled for the dozenth time since leaving the newspaper office. "Can you believe it, Shelby?"

Shelby smirked. "Nope. I can't."

Katy, her hands curled around the steering wheel of Rosemary's car, dared a quick glance at her friend. "Did you say you *can't*?"

Shelby raised one eyebrow. "That's right. I can't believe you left Jonathan Richter off your list of people to tell. After all, he's the one who sent you on this mission in the first place."

Katy jerked her gaze to the road and chewed the inside of her lip. Shelby was right. She needed to tell Jonathan too. She needed to thank him again, not only for telling her about the possibility but also for praying for her. Her stomach fluttered like a million butterflies suddenly burst from their cocoons. Why did she experience both anticipation and apprehension when thinking about talking to Jonathan?

"Of course I'll tell him. When I see him." Katy wouldn't deliberately seek him out. But he might come looking for her since he knew she'd been interviewed that morning. The butterflies multiplied. "But first things first — I need to go home and get those publishing schedule dates on my calendar. I don't want to accidentally miss one of them and disappoint Mr. Matthews."

Shelby propped her arm on the windowsill. The wind tossed her hair, but she didn't seem to mind. "What'll you write about first?"

Katy slowed to turn off the highway onto the dirt road. "The woman who helped me fill out all the paperwork suggested doing a kind of 'meet Katy'-type article for the first one so people would know a little something about me."

"That makes sense," Shelby mused. She tucked her hair behind her ear and wrinkled her nose. "Ugh, dust. I'm rolling this up." She cranked the window closed, and immediately the car felt stuffy. But they were close to home. "Will you ever include your poetry?"

Katy sent Shelby a curious look. "Do you think I should?"

"Duh!" Shelby laughed. "Katy, your poems are amazing. They'd be a great addition to your articles."

Shelby's enthusiasm made Katy smile. "Then maybe I will ..."

They reached Annika's farm. Katy pulled in, as she'd promised to share the news with Annika and her mom. Both of them gave Katy congratulatory hugs, and Annika said, "So what kind of cake do you want? German chocolate? Coconut? Red velvet?"

Katy waved both hands at Annika. "No, no, just something simple. You don't have to go to a lot of trouble."

Annika's mother laughed. "Katy, you know Annika loves to bake, and making a cake for you will be a treat for her as well. It isn't any trouble at all."

"That's right," Annika insisted. "Name your pleasure."

Katy licked her lips, thinking. "Well, if you really mean it, I love that strawberry cake you make that has the cream cheese filling ..."

Annika beamed. "Strawberry cream it is! And — oh!" She slapped both hands to her face, her eyes wide. "I just got the best idea." She spun to grab her mother's hands. "Mom, could we have a party here Friday evening? Invite all the young people and Katy's family — a celebration for Katy becoming a" — she affected a regal pose with raised chin and squinted eyes — "*real, live, published writer?*"

Katy's chest tightened. While she loved that Annika wanted to celebrate on such a grand scale, a party to recognize her accomplishment could be perceived as bragging. "Oh, but — ," she started.

"I think that's a wonderful idea," Mrs. Gehring said over the top of Katy's protest. "We'll have plenty of time to get it organized, and I haven't heard of any other Friday parties this week, so we won't be interfering with someone else's plans." She gave Katy's shoulder a squeeze and smiled. "Katy, you will have the chance to enlighten people to our way of living our faith. Do you realize your articles might eliminate incorrect assumptions and help people see beyond our simple lifestyle to our hearts?"

Tears glittered in Mrs. Gehring's eyes, bringing a sting behind Katy's nose. She gulped. "I — I hadn't really thought of it that way." She'd only seen the newspaper job as a means to fulfill her dream of becoming a writer. But Mrs. Gehring's comments gave her a lot to consider. Drawing in a deep breath, she made a silent vow not to squander the opportunity she'd been given but to use it wisely.

Annika walked Katy to the door. "Be here Friday at seven. I'll invite all our friends, and you invite your family." She gave Katy another hug. "It'll be a wonderful party, Katy — wait and see!"

Dad wasn't home when the girls arrived, so Katy and Shelby told Rosemary about Katy's new job and the party the Gehrings wanted to throw in her honor. Rosemary expressed exuberant congratulations and then said, "As much as I'd like to host the party myself, it might be better if the Gehrings do it. Then it won't be seen as self-promotion."

While they talked, Shelby sat at the kitchen table and chopped tomatoes, cucumbers, and green onions straight from the Lambrights' large garden to add to the lettuce Katy tore into bite-size pieces for a salad. Rosemary spooned homemade ham spread on toast and peeked at the girls over her shoulder. "After lunch, why don't you go to town to let your grandparents and uncle and aunt know. I'm sure Ben and Ruthie will want to come, and I hope they'll bring the children, even if Rebecca isn't up to it."

The reminder of Aunt Rebecca's battle cast a pall over Katy's excitement. Her hands stilled in their task. "How many more chemo treatments will Aunt Rebecca have?"

Rosemary shrugged, bunching her black ribbons against her shoulders. "I believe they plan on eight treatments. Then they'll run some tests. If things look good, they'll stop, but if they still have concerns, she may need more." She shook her head and released a sigh. "She still has a ways to go, I'm afraid. I wish the treatments weren't so hard on her."

Shelby scooped chopped tomatoes into the salad bowl. "But what about Katy and school? I mean, if her aunt is still sick when school starts, is there somebody else who can run the fabric shop? Or will Rebecca just close it until she's ready to go back to work?"

Rosemary turned from the counter and shot a startled look in Shelby's direction. "School?"

Shelby nodded, her puzzled gaze flicking between Katy and Rosemary. "Well, yeah. Katy's not done yet. I mean, she hasn't graduated. So I wondered ..." Her face turned bright pink. She ducked her head and started hacking at a cucumber. "I'm sorry. I shouldn't have asked."

Rosemary slowly approached the table, her face troubled. "No, I'm glad you asked. We've been so caught up thinking about Rebecca ..." She placed her hand on Katy's shoulder. "We've kind of forgotten about school. But we need to think about it."

Katy went back to tearing lettuce. If Rosemary didn't believe a knife would bruise the tender leaves, Katy would be done already. "I know they can't just *close* the shop," she explained to Shelby. "Uncle Albert had a bad fever when he was a boy. It weakened his heart. That's why Dad took over Grampa's dairy. Uncle Albert works part-time as a clerk for the hardware store, but they rely mostly on Aunt Rebecca's income from the fabric shop to support their family." She turned to Rosemary again. "We'll figure something out. Don't worry."

Rosemary squeezed Katy's shoulder and moved back to the counter. She picked up another slice of toast. "Your dad and I will certainly discuss this, Katy. I think you're right that the shop needs to stay open if at all possible, but maybe ..." She sighed and offered a smile. "Well, no need to worry about it right now. We'll find a workable solution. I promise."

But no one else knows what goes on at the fabric shop. And we're running out of time. Katy's hands shook as she tore the last leaves and dropped the pieces into the bowl. Her thoughts turned into a prayer. *God, I want to help my family, but does it have to mean letting go of my dreams?*

❖

After the girls went to Schellberg to share the good news of Katy's writing job with her family, they returned to the farm and Shelby spent the remainder of the afternoon text-messaging with friends from Salina while Katy worked on her first article for the *Free Bee*. By the time Dad and Caleb finished milking, Katy was satisfied with the introductory article. She promised to read it aloud to Shelby before bed, and the girls went down to supper.

Rosemary had prepared an extra-special dinner — roast beef with new potatoes, whole baby onions, and sweet carrots — instead of their customary weeknight casserole, and they ate in the dining room rather than at the kitchen table, adding to the festivity. Dad asked the blessing for the food, and then he added, "Our Father, we thank You for the opportunity Katy's been given to share her faith with others through her writing. Please give her words that will bring glory and honor to You. Amen."

Katy's heart expanded so much she wondered if her chest would be able to hold it. How wonderful to have Dad's support for her writing venture. She took a crusty roll from the bowl and passed them on to Shelby before reaching for the meat platter.

"Everything looks so good," Shelby said.

"Since Katy's big party isn't until Friday," Rosemary said, scooping potatoes onto her plate, "I wanted to do a little something right away. She's earned a special dinner."

The warmth of Rosemary's kindness washed over Katy, and she finally found the courage to do what she'd often felt since the woman became her stepmother. Bouncing out of her chair, she rounded the table and hugged Rosemary. "Thank you for being so sweet to me. I really appreciate you."

Rosemary clung to Katy, and she sniffed, letting Katy know the gesture had touched her deeply. Then she gave her a pat and set her aside. She pointed to Katy's empty chair and said, half-crying, half-laughing, "Go sit down now and let me eat. I already salted these vegetables enough."

Katy laughed and slipped back into her chair. As soon as their plates were filled, she turned to Dad. "Annika told me Caleb asked permission to go to high school. Did you know about it?"

Dad paused midbite. "Yes, the elders informed me he'd asked about going." He put the piece of roast in his mouth.

"So will they let him go?" Katy asked.

Dad swallowed and pinned Katy with a firm look. "That isn't our business, Katy."

Caleb's going would change so many things for Katy.

Didn't that make it her business? But she knew better than
to argue with Dad. Instead, she turned her attention to her
plate. Her enjoyment of the meal chased away questions
about Caleb. When they'd finished, Rosemary brought out
a tray holding four bowls of shortcakes and fresh strawber-
ries buried beneath mounds of sweet whipped cream.

Shelby groaned. "Oh, that looks fantastic. But I'm so
full, I don't think I can eat it."

Rosemary laughed and set the tray on the table. "It'll
keep for a little while if you want to let your dinner settle."
She passed the bowls around. "And maybe while we eat
dessert, we can come up with some ideas about the man-
aging of Rebecca's fabric shop."

Dad dipped his spoon into the dessert. "We can sure
talk about it, but —" He blew out a big breath. "Katy, I
don't want you to get your hopes too high. Aunt Rebecca
needs you. She *trusts* you. You know how important the
shop is for Albert and Rebecca, but just as important right
now is Rebecca's peace of mind. With her being so weak
and sick, we don't want to give her extra reason to worry."

Katy nodded. "The *last* thing I want to do is worry Aunt
Rebecca." And she meant it. She licked a bit of whipped
cream from her thumb and said, "I honestly don't want to
abandon her, Dad. I just need to know ..."

Longing rose up, nearly strangling her. She wanted to
go to school. She wanted to keep learning. Why did God
give her this thirst for knowledge if she wasn't meant to
quench it? She swallowed hard, trying to push the wave of
emotion back down before it emerged in tears. This wasn't
a time for tears.

" ... how long I'll be running the shop on my own.

Because school starts in mid-August. If I'm not going back, I—I'd just like to know. So I can ..." She wanted to say, "Prepare myself emotionally," but she didn't think Dad would understand. So she kept the final words inside.

Rosemary fixed Katy with a serious look. "Which of your friends might be interested in taking on a part-time job?"

Katy lifted her shoulders in a shrug. "So many of them already have jobs. Annika's the only one who's finished with school but not working for someone. She just helps her mom with their housework." Her heart pattered with hope. Would Mr. and Mrs. Gehring release Annika to take a job in town? With so many younger siblings, they depended on Annika quite a bit.

Dad put down his spoon and cupped his hand over Katy's wrist. Very gently, he said, "Katy, unless we can locate someone immediately who is willing to learn to run the shop *and* who meets your aunt's approval, you'll have to accept the possibility that you won't be going to school this fall."

Katy sucked in a sharp breath. Even though she'd suspected Dad would say something similar, it was a lot harder hearing it out loud than she'd imagined.

"After all," Dad went on quietly, "taking care of Aunt Rebecca is more important, isn't it?"

Katy couldn't deny the importance of caring for her aunt. Her family was dear to her; she didn't want to disappoint them. But school was important too. Couldn't someone understand that? Her heart hurt. She offered a weak nod of agreement.

Dad released Katy's hand. "Here's what I'll do ... I'll

visit with Uncle Albert and Aunt Rebecca. I'll suggest
Annika as a possible employee, and I'll also ask for their
suggestions on anyone who might be able to help. After we
explore a little bit, we'll know for sure about sending you
back to school. All right?"

Even though Katy preferred knowing right now, she
couldn't argue. Dad wasn't a magician — he couldn't pro-
duce a manager for the shop any more than he could make
Aunt Rebecca's cancer disappear. "All right, Dad."

Rosemary said, "And of course your dad and I will be
praying for God's will."

"Me too," Shelby put in. "You can count on it."

Katy smiled her thanks.

Rosemary sent a bright smile and wink across the table.
"Everything will work for the best, Katy. You'll see."

Katy wished she had Rosemary's confidence. She
started to thank them for their support, but someone
knocked on the front door. In unison, Dad, Rosemary,
Shelby, and Katy jerked their heads to look in the direction
of the sound. Then Dad, Rosemary, and Shelby all looked
at Katy.

Dad smirked. "I wonder who that could be?"

Shelby snickered. "Betcha I know."

Rosemary dabbed her mouth with her napkin and rose.
"I'll prepare another bowl of strawberry shortcake. Katy,
why don't you answer the door?"

Chapter Eighteen

Katy's hand trembled as it connected with the doorknob and she gave it a twist. The door creaked open, and Jonathan stood on the porch. She could tell by the beaming smile on his face he'd already heard the news.

He reached out and caught both of her hands, squeezing hard. "Congratulations!"

He's holding my hands. If any other boy had been so bold — so open — with her, she'd have fallen over in shock. But holding Jonathan's hands felt natural. Right. The wonder of the moment made Katy giddy. She hunched her shoulders and giggled. "Thank you." They stood for several seconds — her inside, him out — with their linked hands creating a bridge across the threshold and their eyes locked on each other.

"Katy?" Dad's voice interrupted. "Is it Jonathan?"

"Yes, Dad," Katy called. Reluctantly, she pulled her hands free of Jonathan's.

"Well, bring him in." Dad sounded amused.

Katy wished she could pinch her father. But of course she couldn't. So she said very politely, "Won't you come in, Jonathan? We're having strawberry shortcake."

Jonathan snatched his bill cap from his head as he stepped over the threshold. Katy closed the door then gestured for Jonathan to follow her to the dining room. They reached the table just as Rosemary hurried in from the kitchen with a fresh bowl of dessert. She sent Jonathan a beaming smile.

"Welcome! Have a seat there by Katy." She put the bowl, a spoon, and a napkin at the open spot and then returned to her own chair.

Jonathan greeted everyone before looping his hat on the chair's back. But instead of sitting, he held his hand to Katy's chair. Her ears heated with pleasure. "Th-thank you," she said. She slipped into her chair. Only then did Jonathan seat himself. The sweet scent of the strawberry shortcake beckoned to her, but she couldn't eat. Having Jonathan so close made her stomach feel too full to hold anything else.

He dug into his dessert, though, and ate every bit while Katy told him about the interview at the newspaper. Then he visited with Dad about horses, the differences between Schellberg and his fellowship in Pennsylvania, and cars. Katy listened, intrigued not so much by the topics but by Jonathan's communication skills. He was articulate and confident, seemingly comfortable talking to Dad even though they were a generation apart in age and he wasn't a member of the fellowship. Her admiration for him grew greater by the minute.

Suddenly he turned and looked at her. "I understand there's a party at the Gehrings on Friday night to congratulate you on your new job."

Up close, his eyes were piercingly blue. Katy gulped.

"Th-that's right. It was Annika's idea." She hoped Jonathan wouldn't think she'd asked for the party. Several months ago, she'd heard that some of the Schellberg boys considered her self-important because she enjoyed using an extensive vocabulary and attended public high school. If Jonathan ever thought her conceited, it would break her heart.

His smile remained. "I plan to be there — Yvonne and I were invited. And then ..." His lips quivered, as if fighting a battle not to frown. "On Saturday, Dan and Sandra will take me to the bus station in Salina and send me back to Pennsylvania."

Shelby burst out, "What? Already?"

Jonathan nodded. Disappointment dimmed his eyes. "I came to help with the corn harvest. And it'll be done by the end of the week. So ..."

Katy's chest tightened. She couldn't draw a breath. Without air, she couldn't speak. She sat in silence, battling tears. Why did his leaving bother her so much?

Rosemary said, "I'm sorry to see you go, Jonathan. We've enjoyed your company these past weeks."

Jonathan's Adam's apple bobbed in a swallow. "I've enjoyed being in Schellberg. It's a great town." He chuckled, ducking his head for a moment. "At first I liked it because I could drive. Driving a car is very different than driving a buggy. But I guess that's a pretty selfish reason for liking a place."

Katy remembered thinking the same thing when Yvonne mentioned Jonathan's enjoyment of driving. But that was before she'd met him. Now that she knew him, she knew he wasn't selfish. Not at all.

"But now that I know the people," Jonathan continued, as if reading Katy's thoughts, "I like Schellberg for a completely different reason." He shifted his head to look directly into Katy's face. "It'll be hard to leave."

Katy stared silently into his eyes. A lump filled her throat. She didn't want him to go.

Dad cleared his throat.

Both Jonathan and Katy jumped. They looked at Dad.

The amused glint Dad seemed to acquire every time Jonathan came around returned. "Maybe we should combine Katy's congratulatory party into a going-away party too."

"Oh, no!" Katy exclaimed then clamped her lips shut. She hadn't meant to holler the thought aloud, but how could she combine a happy event with a sad one and enjoy the evening? She didn't want to even *think* about Jonathan leaving, let alone attend a party commemorating his departure.

Dad gave her a funny look, and she knew he thought she wanted the attention for herself. She needed to clarify, but how could she say something so personal with Jonathan sitting right there? It would have to wait until later. She scrambled for a reason for her outburst.

"It — it wouldn't be fair to Jonathan. He — It — " She stammered to a halt. Why did she lose her ability to speak clearly in this boy's presence?

Jonathan offered a sympathetic smile. "It's okay, Katy. I really don't want a going-away party. Because ..." He drew in a deep breath and faced Dad. "When I get back to Lancaster County, I intend to talk to my folks about changing fellowships and moving to Schellberg for good."

Shelby let out a little shriek. "Really?"

Jonathan's broad grin returned. "Really. Dan and Sandra said I could live with them until I found a place of my own. Mr. Penner said he could use me at his furniture shop. I've never built furniture, but I've helped my brothers build buggies, so I know how to use all the tools. He's willing to give me a try."

"But," Shelby interrupted, "you don't want to be a furniture-maker, you want to be a — " She stopped, looking from Jonathan to Katy as if afraid she'd almost divulged a secret.

Jonathan waved his hand at her. "It's all right. My cousins know I'd like to attend school too." He turned to Dad again. "That's part of the reason I want to change fellowships. Since the Schellberg elders approved Katy to go to school" — he zipped a quick smile at Katy before facing Dad again — "I hoped maybe I'd be allowed to go too. My fellowship is much more traditional. If I stay there, going to a public school will be out of the question. Dan said he'd talk to the elders for me. Of course . . ." He chuckled, raising one eyebrow. "It all depends on what my folks say. If my dad says no, I won't argue with him."

Katy's heart swelled. *Honour thy father and thy mother . . .* The Mennonite fellowships expected children to act in obedience. It warmed her that Jonathan took his faith's teaching so seriously.

Dad folded his hands on the edge of the table. "It sounds as if you're making some big decisions, Jonathan. Rosemary and I will be in prayer for you as you seek God's will for your life."

"I appreciate that, sir." Jonathan pushed away from the

table. "But I've taken up enough of your time this evening.
I really just wanted to tell Katy congratulations and wish
her well, and ..." His expression turned bashful. "Mr.
Lambright, would it be all right if Katy and I stepped out
on the porch for a few minutes?"

Dad gave a little jolt, as if Jonathan's words caught
him by surprise, but then he smiled. The amused, knowing smile that annoyed Katy. "I suppose that would be all
right."

Jonathan said a proper good-bye to Rosemary, Dad, and
Shelby before plucking his hat from the chair back and
gesturing for Katy to precede him to the front room. She
scurried ahead of him, her heart pounding. What did he
want to say that he couldn't say in front of the others?

On the porch, instead of talking to her, Jonathan moved
to the railing. Katy stood to the side, watching him. He
wadded his bill cap in his hand rather than wearing it and
tipped his face to the sky. Although sunset was still an
hour away, a few bright stars already peeked through in
the north, and the undersides of the clouds glowed brighter
than the tops as the sun slinked toward the horizon. The
sky was beautiful, but she preferred to look at Jonathan.
Katy stepped alongside him but didn't say anything, allowing him to enjoy the vast view.

Finally he sighed and shifted to face her. "Katy, I guess
it's no secret that I think you're a very special girl."

No, it isn't a secret. Heat seared Katy's ears. She ducked
her head, uncertain how to respond.

His soft voice went on, so sweet and tender it made
Katy's chest ache in a pleasing way. "I'm not looking for
any kind of promise from you — I think we're too young,

and you need to be focusing on school rather than court-ing—but I wondered if ... maybe ... if I end up moving to Schellberg, if ... someday ..."

Katy swallowed a smile. Girls weren't the only ones who got tongue-tied. Her head still low, she nodded, her ribbons flicking her chin with the rapid movement. "Yes, Jonathan. I think ... maybe ... someday."

He slapped his hat onto his head. "Well, I better go then. See you ... Friday night." He clomped off the porch, charged across the yard, and climbed into Dan Richter's truck. The engine rumbled to life, and Jonathan stuck his hand out the window to wave. Katy got a glimpse of his bright smile before the truck pulled away from the house and headed down the road.

She stood on the porch and watched until he turned the corner and disappeared in a cloud of dust. She stayed, watching, until the dust settled. Then her eyes turned to the same patch of sky Jonathan had been examining. An explosion of colors greeted her eyes, and a poem began to take shape in her mind. She pulled a little spiral notebook and the stub of a pencil from her pocket and scribbled as quickly as she could:

The large ball, turned orange, hangs heavy
in the evening sky.
Colors melt together like crayons left outside
on a summer day—
Blue, gray, pink, yellow, orange—
All accentuated by white-white clouds with silver linings.
As the large ball sinks reluctantly downward,
colors come alive across the sky—

Glorious orange, dazzling pink, blood red,
luminous yellow, radiant blue—
The sun's last, brilliantly futile attempt to defy
darkness of night.
The large ball disappears beyond the horizon,
And gray overtakes the sky.

She reread the poem and then gave it a title: *Farewell, Day*. Tears pricked behind her eyes. No one would ever know how the poem represented the bright joy of her time with Jonathan followed by the gray sadness of his departure. She slipped the notebook into her pocket and returned to the house.

Chapter Nineteen

Tuesday morning, as Katy and Shelby headed out the door to work, Rosemary called, "Girls, I've got leftover roast beef from last night's supper. Would you like me to bring you some sandwiches at lunchtime?"

"That'd be great," Katy said. Without a refrigerator at the shop to keep food from spoiling, she and Shelby hadn't packed a lunch each day but ordered something from the café. She liked the idea of saving her money. "We'll see you later!"

The girls didn't talk much as they headed for town. When they'd gone up to bed last night, Katy had told Shelby the details of her conversation with Jonathan. They'd talked well beyond bedtime. Maybe they'd talked too late, because Katy battled tiredness all morning, and she caught Shelby yawning behind her hand more than once. She intended to go to bed earlier tonight. Being sleepy on the job wasn't very responsible.

The shop bustled with activity, making the morning zip by, and when Rosemary stepped into the shop with a small wicker basket on her arm, Katy looked at the clock above the door in surprise. "It's lunchtime already?"

Rosemary laughed. "Afraid so. Are you hungry?"

"Ravenous," Shelby said. She grabbed her crutches and came out from behind the counter. "For a small town, this place sure rocks with activity!"

Rosemary laughed. She removed wax paper–wrapped packages and jars of tea from the basket. "Well, here, have your lunch. Maybe it'll recharge you for the afternoon."

Just as they perched on the windowsill to eat, the door opened and Mrs. Krehbiel entered the shop. Katy rose to take care of her, but Rosemary waved her hand. "You sit and eat, Katy. I'll see what she needs."

Relieved, Katy sank back down and bit into the sandwich. The combination of roast beef, sweet pickles, and mayonnaise pleased her taste buds. "Mm," she said.

Shelby grinned her agreement. She bobbed her head toward Rosemary and Mrs. Krehbiel, who perused the notions at the far side of the shop. "Your stepmom's a good cook."

"Rosemary's good at a lot of things," Katy confirmed. She took another bite, chewed, and swallowed. "You ought to see the clothes and quilt tops she sews. She sewed for other people for a living before she moved to Schellberg and married my dad."

Shelby's eyes flew wide. She grabbed Katy's arm, dislodging a slice of pickle from Katy's sandwich. "Hey!"

Katy grunted, lifting the pickle from her skirt. A circular stain marked the spot where it had landed. "Shelby, what're you doing?"

Shelby ignored Katy's disgruntled question. "If your stepmom's good at sewing and stuff, why couldn't she work here in the shop? I mean, your aunt would trust her,

wouldn't she? She's family and everything. And if she had
her own sewing business, she'd sure know how to keep
the books and all."

Katy shook her head. "Sure, Aunt Rebecca trusts
Rosemary. They've become good friends. But Rosemary
can't work here."

"Why not?"

Katy sighed. "She already has a full-time job being my
dad's wife. She takes care of the house, sometimes she
helps in the dairy ... Dad wouldn't like the idea of her
coming here every day instead of seeing to her responsibilities at home."

Shelby's shoulders sagged. "Oh. Well ..." She took a bite
of her sandwich and chewed, her gaze aimed across the
shop at Rosemary. "That's too bad. She sure looks like she
knows what she's doing."

Katy watched Rosemary pluck several things from
the pegboard and carry them to the counter, chatting
softly with Mrs. Krehbiel. Again, Katy started to rise, but
Rosemary shook her head.

"I'll get it. Finish eating."

So Katy allowed Rosemary to tally Mrs. Krehbiel's
purchases and make change. She did seem to know what
to do in a shop. But if Dad wanted Rosemary to work,
he'd have said something at the dinner table. Obviously,
he preferred his wife to stay home and see to the needs of
the household. She couldn't blame him, either. He'd gone
many years without a life partner. Katy wouldn't suggest
taking Rosemary away from Dad, even for a short time.
She finished her sandwich as Mrs. Krehbiel headed out the
door with her bag of purchases.

Katy hurried to the counter. "Thanks for taking care of that. It was nice to sit and eat and not worry."

"You're welcome." Rosemary gathered her basket and empty jars. "I'll get out of your way now so you can work. See you girls at home this evening." She bustled out.

The afternoon proved as busy as the morning, and Katy wasn't able to do any cleaning until after she'd put out the CLOSED sign. Her stomach rumbled while she ran the vacuum cleaner, and she could hardly wait to get home and eat. She hoped Rosemary had prepared a big dinner. She hurried into the back room to put the vacuum cleaner in the storage corner then heaved a sigh, eager to go home. Just then a knocking sound carried from the front—obviously a fist on the door.

Katy groaned. If a customer needed something, she'd have to let them in—Aunt Rebecca tried to accommodate people. But she really wanted to leave. She scurried out to the front. Instead of a customer, she found Uncle Albert peering through the window. Gramma Ruthie stood beside him. Their faces wore matching somber expressions.

Shelby pointed. She looked worried. "What do you think they need?"

Katy's heart fired into her throat. "I don't know." She twisted the lock and flung the door open. "What is it? Is Aunt Rebecca all right?"

Uncle Albert and Gramma stepped inside. Uncle Albert headed straight for the back room, and Gramma said quietly, "Katy, lock the door, then come here. We need to talk."

Katy sent a frightened look to Shelby then gave the lock a twist and headed for the counter where Gramma waited. Uncle Albert emerged from the back room with three folding chairs. He clanked them open in a circle and said, "Have a seat."

Shelby stayed on the tall stool behind the counter, and Gramma, Uncle Albert, and Katy each chose a chair. Katy braced her hands on her knees. To distract herself she tapped her thumb on the little circle stain left by the pickle at lunchtime. "What is it? What's wrong with Aunt Rebecca?"

Uncle Albert spoke. "Your aunt isn't recovering like she ought to, Katy. With the medicine the doctor gave her, she should be able to regain enough strength between treatments to get up and move around some. But she won't try. She just lies there and refuses to do anything."

Katy shook her head, concerned. That didn't sound like Aunt Rebecca.

Uncle Albert glanced at Gramma Ruthie. "We talked to the doctor on the telephone today. He says her blood cell and enzyme counts look good. The medicine she's taking should relieve her tiredness. So he thinks her problem isn't physical as much as it is emotional."

Katy crinkled her brow. "Emotional?"

Gramma put her hand over Katy's. "The doctor thinks she's depressed, Katy-girl."

Uncle Albert continued. "She won't come here because she said she isn't needed — everyone has told her what a good job you and Shelby are doing." He pulled his lips into a sour line. "We thought we were assuring her by telling her she wasn't needed, but now I'm thinking we made a mistake. Rebecca's a strong, independent woman. Although she isn't prideful, I know she tries to be like the woman in Proverbs 31 who takes care of her family and her business."

He sighed. "Since she got sick, she hasn't had any responsibility at all. Your gramma sees to the house and children. You see to the shop. So Rebecca doesn't have a reason to get off that sofa and do anything. She just lies there, feeling sorry for herself."

Katy held her hands outward. "What can I do?"

Uncle Albert and Gramma Ruthie exchanged a meaningful look. Then Gramma squeezed Katy's hand. "Katy-girl, we need you to *stop* doing."

Katy sent a puzzled glance at Shelby. Shelby raised her shoulders, expressing her own confusion.

Uncle Albert added, "If we're going to get Rebecca off that sofa and back into life, we've got to give her a good reason to get up. We can't use housework as a reason. She knows Lori and Lola can handle the housework, because they've been doing it for over a year already. As much as she loves this shop, it's the only thing we can think of. If she loses your help, she won't have a choice. She'll *have* to come in."

"B-but," Katy spluttered, "I can't lie to her!" Dad would never agree to let her be intentionally deceitful, not even to motivate Aunt Rebecca. And she didn't want to be deceptive. It went against her conscience.

"Katy, we're not asking you to lie," Gramma Ruthie said. "We're asking you to be willing to step aside and make room for Rebecca to be in charge again. You just got that new job with the newspaper. Rebecca was asleep the other day when you and Shelby came by, so she didn't hear the news. At first we didn't want to tell her because we didn't want her to worry that you might leave the shop. But we've changed our minds."

Uncle Albert gave a firm nod. "That's right. At the doctor's recommendation, we're going to tell her about it this evening. She knows how much writing means to you, so we hope she'll decide on her own to come in and let you put more attention on your writing job. Do you see?"

Katy's heart pattered. If their plan worked — if Aunt Rebecca returned to the shop even part-time — then Katy wouldn't need to spend so many hours here. The promise of free time danced in her mind. She might even be able to return to school! She closed her eyes. *God, don't let me be selfish. Let me make the right choice for the right reason.* Suddenly she remembered the difficult days when she worried about whether Dad would still need her if he took a wife. She wouldn't wish the feeling of being unneeded on anybody.

Opening her eyes, she looked at Uncle Albert's apprehensive face. "I'll do whatever I can to help Aunt Rebecca feel needed again."

Uncle Albert blew out a huge breath and a relieved smile removed his worried look. He wrapped Katy in a hug. "I knew we could count on you, Katy-girl." He kissed her cheek and set her aside. "C'mon, Mom, let's go break this news to my wife." He bowed his head and crunched his eyes closed. "Dear Lord, please let this work. Bring my feisty wife back to me."

Gramma Ruthie, Katy, and Shelby all echoed, "Amen."

❖

Wednesday afternoon, Katy was in the middle of cutting a length of fabric for Mrs. Ensz and her daughter when the door opened and Aunt Rebecca stepped into the shop.

Katy stifled a gasp. She hadn't seen her aunt for several days, but it appeared she'd lost even more weight. With no hair to fill her mesh headcovering, her cap looked too big for her head, and her dress hung on her frame. Her face looked pale, even more frail since her eyelashes and eyebrows had also fallen out. But her eyes snapped with a determination Katy well remembered.

Katy forced a smile and tried to act as if Aunt Rebecca entered the shop every afternoon. "Hi."

Aunt Rebecca put her hands on her hips and looked around without replying.

Shelby waved from her spot behind the counter. "Good afternoon."

A little grunt served as her aunt's reply.

Mrs. Ensz bustled to Aunt Rebecca and embraced her. "It's so good to see you up, Rebecca! We've missed you at services." She kept her hands on Aunt Rebecca's shoulders and seemed to examine her. "But we need to fatten you up. Would you like me to bring over my chicken-cheese enchiladas for your supper tonight?"

Katy cringed. She knew Mrs. Ensz meant well, but Aunt Rebecca's weak stomach would never handle the rich enchiladas the woman brought to nearly every church dinner.

"That's kind of you, Lucinda, but my girls already have our supper planned." Aunt Rebecca stepped away from Mrs. Ensz's hands.

"Well, what helpful girls you have," Mrs. Ensz said. "It sounds as if you're very well cared for."

"Yes, I am very well cared for." Aunt Rebecca's lips formed a firm line.

As soon as Mrs. Ensz paid Shelby for her purchases and headed out the door with her little girl skipping alongside her, Aunt Rebecca whirled on Katy.

"Young lady, I have a bone to pick with you."

Katy gulped. "Y-yes?"

"I hear you're leaving me."

What had Uncle Albert told her? Katy wished she'd been in on the conversation so she had some clue how to respond. She stuttered out a weak reply. "N-not really. I mean, I can still work here, if you need me."

Aunt Rebecca released a soft laugh. Her eyes crinkled with affection. "Ah, Katy-girl, you are always so obliging ..."

She crossed to the counter and rested her arm on its smooth, dust-free top. Standing there, leaning on the counter as if for support, she looked pale and delicate and yet somehow strong and capable at the same time. The sight put a lump in Katy's throat.

"I do still need you, Katy. But I haven't been fair, leaving everything to you. This shop ..." Her gaze traveled the room slowly, as if reacquainting herself with the contents. "It isn't your dream—it's mine. And when a person lets go of her dream, she hurts herself." She zinged a frown at Katy. "I don't intend to let you make the same mistake. Not to take care of me."

Katy held her breath.

"I can't be here all the time yet. I don't have the strength." Aunt Rebecca lifted her chin. "But I intend to come in a little bit each day to rebuild my stamina. It won't be long, and I'll be back at the helm."

Katy didn't want to sound eager to leave, so she didn't ask when Aunt Rebecca thought that might be. Instead, she offered a bright smile. "That sounds good, Aunt Rebecca. I've missed you." With a start, she realized how much she had missed her saucy, independent, opinionated aunt. But she also liked the softer, more affectionate side that had been creeping into view. She hoped Aunt Rebecca would hold onto the best of both halves of her when she was finally well again.

Aunt Rebecca sighed. "I'd like to stay today, but the walk to town wore me out. I need to go home. But I plan to come in tomorrow, and I will definitely be at your party Friday night." She smiled, her eyes glittering. "It'll be good to be among my friends and family — a part of everyone's life again."

Katy dashed across the floor and hugged her aunt. Not hard — she feared she might break something, Aunt Rebecca was so thin — but with heart. Aunt Rebecca returned the hug and then moved to the door. "Good-bye, girls. I'll see you tomorrow." She stepped outside.

Shelby clapped and let out a whoop. "Katy! It worked! She's up! She walked all the way to town on her own!" She laughed. "It's like a miracle!"

Katy nodded. "I know. It's amazing." She stared after Aunt Rebecca, gratitude making her heart pound.

Shelby said, "And just think! If she gets her strength back like she wants, she might very well be ready to take this place over again by the time school starts. Which means — "

Katy held up her hand. "Don't say it! I don't want to start wishing, just in case it doesn't happen."

Shelby laughed again. "Okay, I guess I understand. But,

girlfriend, just so you know — I'm gonna be wishing hard enough for both of us!"

Katy bit down on her lower lip for a moment. How she treasured Shelby's friendship. Almost holding her breath, she said, "Shelby, if what we want doesn't happen — if I can't go back to school for some reason — do you think we'll still be friends?"

Shelby's eyes flew wide. "Why wouldn't we be?"

Katy shrugged. "Well, we see each other at school. And if I'm not there ..."

Shelby slipped off the chair, grabbed her crutches, and stumped across the floor to Katy. Flinging one arm around Katy's neck, she hugged her tight. "Katy, don't you know by now it isn't school that makes us friends? You and me — we're connected! BFF, that's us."

Katy, caught in Shelby's embrace, smiled. *Best friends forever.* She returned Shelby's hug and then tugged loose. "But it won't be easy to stay friends. What with me here, you there, and no telephone or anything so we can communicate."

"Friends find a way," Shelby insisted. She limped back behind the counter and climbed onto the stool. "So don't sweat it. You're stuck with me, Katy Lambright."

Katy decided to believe Shelby. It was nice to have one thing in her life that wasn't changing.

Chapter Twenty

Katy's congratulatory party turned into a welcome-back party for Aunt Rebecca, but Katy didn't mind a bit. Although her aunt spent most of the evening sitting in a chair in the shade, allowing people to come to her rather than mingling, she laughed and talked and seemed to enjoy herself. It gave Katy's heart a lift to see the smiles on Aunt Rebecca's, Uncle Albert's, and their children's faces after the weeks of worry and melancholy. Even though they still had a big battle to fight, they were armed with happiness and hope, and Katy held tight to both.

She tried to talk to everyone in attendance at least once so they would know how much she appreciated them coming and celebrating with her, but she kept finding her way back to Jonathan's side. She told herself it was because he was leaving and he might not be back. After all, there were no guarantees his parents would approve his return to Schellberg. If she didn't take time for him now, she might not get another chance. But deep down, she knew the truth. She enjoyed his company, and she wanted to spend time with him.

Jonathan didn't seem to mind her showing up again and again. He welcomed her with a smile each time, excused himself from conversation with whoever else was nearby, and gave her his full attention. She wondered if he held the same thought as she—grab their moments while they could. Either way, she appreciated the way he made her feel special and wanted.

Midway through the evening, Katy made her way to the cake table for a second slice of strawberry cream cake. Annika had made sure Katy got the first piece as soon as she arrived at the party, and Katy had savored every bite. But that was over an hour ago and she was ready for another piece. To her dismay, the platter only held crumbs. She put her hand on her hip and huffed.

"What's wrong?" Caleb's familiar voice came from behind Katy.

Without turning around, she pointed to the crumb-scattered platter. "I was hoping for another piece, but I'm too late. It's all gone."

Caleb stepped beside her. A self-conscious grin creased his freckled face. "I guess I'm responsible for that." He held up his plate. A towering slab of strawberry cream cake filled the center of the plate and even hung off on one side.

Katy gawked. "That's the biggest piece of cake I've ever seen!"

Caleb laughed. "Yeah, well, strawberry cake is my favorite."

Katy sighed, looking with longing at the contents of Caleb's plate. "Mine too. Annika baked it especially for me." Not until the words left her lips did she consider how manipulative they sounded. She added quickly, "But it was meant to be shared. You're welcome to it."

Caleb looked at the cake and then at Katy. His expression turned contrite. "I don't really need this much. Here." He put the plate on the table, picked up a knife, and cut the piece into two slices. He tipped one slice onto a clean plate and held it Katy. "Enjoy."

Katy shook her head, amazed. Caleb Penner being unselfishly gallant. What would happen next?

Caleb stabbed his fork into the cake and brought up a huge bite. "I guess you've heard I asked to go to high school this fall."

Katy nodded but didn't reply. She was too busy chewing, and unlike some people, she refused to talk around a bite of food.

"Still haven't got an answer from the elders," he said, jabbing his fork into the cake again. "But I think I've just about changed my mind anyway."

Two other boys approached the cake table, so she moved out of the way. Caleb followed. Katy laid her fork on the edge of her plate and tipped her head, giving Caleb a curious look. "Why did you want to go? You never seemed to like school all that much."

Caleb scowled. "I don't like school all that much. Not the studying part, anyway. But you know when we all went bowling? I talked with your friend Cora, and she told me about all the stuff that goes on at high school—you know, the sports teams and clubs and stuff. A lot more fun than our little school. And"—he shoved another good-sized bite into his mouth, chomped down a few times, and swallowed—"I guess I kinda hoped it would give you and me something in ... I dunno ... common." His freckles disappeared underneath a red blush.

Katy suddenly lost her appetite for the cake. "Caleb ..."

He hurried on. "I know we've had our disagreements, and I've been really stupid sometimes. I don't know why I tease so much."

Katy did, but she wouldn't say it out loud.

"But I kinda hoped you could forget all that and ... I dunno ... let me come around as more than just your dad's hired hand?"

Katy looked into his eager face. She could look at Caleb without wanting to sock him on the arm anymore. That was progress. And there were good reasons to say yes to his request. But she couldn't seem to form the word. She searched her heart, trying to find the reason for her reluctance. Was it because she hoped she might be able to spend time with Jonathan instead, or was it something else? And she finally realized the truth.

"Caleb, I'm glad we're finally really getting to be friends. I didn't like feeling mad at you all the time. It's nice that we can talk to each other and be relaxed." His expression didn't change. Katy drew in a fortifying breath and continued. "But honestly, I don't think I can look at you as more than a friend. We've spent too much time together, I guess. When I look at you, I see a ... brother."

He scowled. "A *brother*?"

She nodded. Obviously, she'd offended him, but she had to be honest. It was the only fair thing to do. "You know how brothers and sisters squabble when they're growing up?"

As if to prove her point, two of Annika's younger brothers dashed by, the one in the lead laughing uproariously and the one following vowing to get even. Caleb watched them go. A funny grin twitched his cheek. "Yeah. I know."

"Well, that's been us since we started school. Teasing. Squabbling. Getting mad at each other." She shrugged. "We're growing up now, so we're finally getting past all that" — *thank goodness!* — "which is nice, but us as something more than friends . . . ?"

Months ago, when Caleb had asked to date her and she'd told him she didn't want to be his girlfriend, he'd gotten angry and said hurtful things. She didn't want to face his anger again. It would spoil her special evening. She gathered her courage and finished. "I don't think so, Caleb."

He sucked in his lips and stared off to the side.

Katy tipped her head, trying to catch his eye. "Are you mad?"

Seconds passed. The mingled voices of her friends and family carried across the yard and covered the sound of her pounding heart. When he still didn't say anything, she repeated, "Caleb, are you mad?"

He finally sighed and looked at her. "Not mad, Katydid. Just kind of . . . I dunno . . . sad."

Katy nodded. It hurt to let someone go when you cared about them. She'd had a hard time telling Bryce she couldn't be more than friends with him — it felt like a good-bye to possibilities. And saying good-bye to Jonathan tonight would be even harder. "I'm sorry. I don't mean to hurt you."

"Hey, you were honest." He used a glib tone, but Katy saw hurt lingering in his eyes. "Can't blame a guy for trying, right?" He shrugged and dropped his plate, still holding a few bites of cake, onto the end of the table. He snorted out a brief laugh. "But dating a sister is just plain gross. So I'm outta here. See you, Katy." He ambled off toward a cluster of boys at the edge of the yard. As soon as he reached them, he punched the closest one on the arm and joined their conversation as if nothing was wrong.

Katy smiled. Caleb would be all right. She reached for her cake again.

"Katy! Katy!" Annika's voice captured her attention.

She turned and spotted her friend waving for Katy to join her, Shelby, and a few other girls at a picnic table near the porch. She hesitated — where was Jonathan right now? — but then she remembered how much it had bothered her when Shelby ignored Katy to spend all her time with her boyfriend last year. Cake plate in hand, she moved to the table.

"Guess what?" Yvonne said as soon as Katy joined the group. "Annika's going to start working at the café."

Katy gawked at the girl. "What!" She spun to face Annika. "Your folks are letting you take a job?"

"Just part-time," Annika said. "I'm going to go in early in the mornings and bake cakes. Isn't it great?" She looked like she might burst from happiness. "I get to do what I love to do and even get paid for it!"

Katy understood Annika's excitement. She gave her friend a huge hug. "Annika, that's great! I'm so happy for you!" And she was, even though she realized it meant Annika wouldn't be available to work at Aunt Rebecca's shop. Oddly, worry didn't strike. Rosemary and Dad had assured her things would work out. She and Shelby were praying. Maybe the fact that she was able to trust God with her desire to attend school meant she was growing up. She liked the idea.

Annika wriggled loose from Katy's grasp, and her eyes twinkled with fun. "Sit down and listen. We've got some ideas for your future articles."

Katy laughed until her stomach hurt as the girls tossed out various topics, mostly ludicrous. From a nearby table, more laughter rolled — Aunt Rebecca, Uncle Albert, and Annika's mother. A verse from Proverbs, *"A merry heart doeth good like a medicine,"* flitted through Katy's mind, and she realized how true it was. The worry of the past weeks melted away on a flood of happiness.

At nine o'clock, people began loading into their vehicles to leave. Katy stood near the driveway to say good-bye to everyone and thank them again for coming. Yvonne and Jonathan were among the last to leave. Yvonne bid Katy farewell and best wishes on her new job then said, "Let's go, Jonathan."

But Jonathan held back. "Go ahead — I'll be there in a minute."

Yvonne opened her mouth as if she wanted to argue but then she shrugged. "All right."

Jonathan waited until she moved out of earshot. "Katy, when I get home, is it okay if I send you letters?" He released a self-conscious laugh, running his hand through his hair. "I'm not much of a writer — not like you — but I'd like to keep in touch, if you don't mind."

Did he suspect he wouldn't be back? Katy wished she

had the courage to ask the question. She pasted on a bright smile and nodded. "I'd like that. We can be pen pals."

"At least for a while," he said, and then she knew he hoped for more too. He shoved his hands into his trouser pockets and rocked on his heels a couple of times. A sweet smile tipped up his lips. "'Bye, Katy."

❖

The last week of July flew by. Katy and Shelby continued to work all day in the fabric shop, but Aunt Rebecca came in every day except her chemotherapy days and spent the afternoon with them. Although she lacked her previous energy, she regained enough strength to get bossy. But Katy wasn't insulted. It was good to see glimpses of the old Aunt Rebecca.

On Friday, Aunt Rebecca released the girls early with instructions not to come in at all on Saturday.

"Are you sure?" Katy asked.

"I'm sure. Aren't Shelby's parents coming for her tomorrow?" Aunt Rebecca asked.

Both girls affected a pout and then laughed. Shelby answered, "Yes. They texted me this morning that they're back in the United States. They're exhausted from the travel, so I told them to sleep as long as they wanted to and come get me when they felt rested."

"Which will be tomorrow afternoon sometime," Katy said. It would be hard to let Shelby leave. She'd enjoyed having a sister. But she knew Shelby was eager to see her family again. Katy couldn't imagine being apart from Dad for six whole weeks.

"Then just enjoy your morning together," Aunt Rebecca said.

Katy hesitated. It didn't seem responsible to leave Aunt Rebecca all alone in the shop, even if it was just for a Saturday morning. "But won't you need some extra hands?"

Aunt Rebecca sent Katy a firm look. "Katy, if you must know, I'll have some extra hands tomorrow. Joanne Krehbiel is coming in."

Katy drew back in surprise. "Joanne? But she works at the grocery store in Salina."

"She does," Aunt Rebecca said, "but she's tired of the drive and is thinking about making a change. So I told her she could come spend a few hours with me and see if she'd like working here instead." A funny little smile teased the corners of Aunt Rebecca's mouth. "If I hire her, it'll mean you're out of a job. Would that disappoint you?"

Katy clasped her hands to keep from socking the air in excitement. "I think I could live with it."

Aunt Rebecca laughed then sobered. "I don't know for sure it will work out, but if it does . . ."

Katy didn't need to hear anymore. She sucked in a long breath and held it. *Please, God?*

Aunt Rebecca wrapped Shelby in a hug. "Thank you for your help this summer, Shelby. You have been a blessing to both Katy and me."

Shelby couldn't hug back with her hands on her crutches, but she leaned into the embrace. "You're welcome. I've had fun!"

The girls headed to Caleb's cart. Neither spoke until Katy guided Rocky out of town. Then Shelby sighed. "Can you believe summer's almost over?"

"It sure went fast," Katy said.

"*Too* fast," Shelby added.

Katy sent a sidelong, apologetic glance at Shelby. "We didn't get to do most of what we wanted to do."

Shelby shrugged. "Not a big deal. I know where you live—and once I get rid of my cast and can drive again, I can come out some Saturday." She grinned. "We'll pester Annika to teach me to write my name in calligraphy or spend the afternoon with your grandma. I can't do a whole quilt in an afternoon, but at least I'd get a lesson, right?"

"Right," Katy said. Even though she wasn't certain she'd get to return to school, she still clung to the hope that she'd be able to go. But if she didn't, Shelby would still come out and see her. She wouldn't lose the precious friendship.

"You know, Katy, I was thinking about something." Shelby's tone turned musing. "Your purpose in finishing high school was so you could go to college and become a journalist, right?"

Katy nodded, giving the reins a pull to guide Rocky around the corner. "Right."

"Well, it occurs to me you've already accomplished the goal. I mean, by writing for the *Free Bee*. So, if something should happen—not that I want something to happen, but just 'if,' okay?—you can still tell people, 'I'm a journalist.' Because you are." Shelby sat forward and pinned Katy with a serious look. "Do you see what I'm saying?"

Katy understood. She gave Shelby a big smile. "I see. Thanks."

Shelby settled back in the seat. "Good. Now, can we go

by the pasture and see the horses one more time? I just love stroking the white spot on Saydee's sweet nose."

Katy laughed. "Sure! C'mon, Rocky, let's go visit Shadow and Saydee."

While Shelby petted Saydee, Katy caught herself looking for Jonathan to show up. Somehow the pasture seemed empty without him. The thought made her sad, and she didn't want to be sad on Shelby's last day in Schellberg.

"We better go," Katy said.

Shelby said her good-byes to the horses, and the girls returned to the cart. As they rolled into Katy's yard, Dad stepped out of the barn. He trotted over to meet them.

"Did Aunt Rebecca talk to you about Joanne Krehbiel?"

Hope flickered in Katy's heart. She nodded.

Shelby pressed her clasped hands beneath her chin. "Mr. Lambright, does that mean Katy'll be able to finish school? I mean, I know having someone to fill in at the fabric shop's only part of it — she needs permission from the deacons too — but ..."

Katy bit down on her lower lip, watching Dad's face. Once again Shelby had impulsively jumped in. Would Dad be offended?

Dad rubbed his finger under his nose, his head low. Then he looked directly at Shelby, as if Katy wasn't even sitting on the cart seat beside her. "I don't see any reason why the deacons would refuse to let her go. She was told she'd be kept home if she began picking up worldly habits or we feared for her spiritual well-being." His gaze shifted to settle on Katy. The tenderness and pride in his eyes made Katy's chest swell. "Those fears have been put to rest."

"Yahoo!" Shelby threw her arm around Katy's shoulders and squeezed. "You'll be back, girlfriend. I just *know* it!"

Dad reached for the reins. "I'll put the horse in the corral for you. Go on in and eat." His eyes twinkled. "I picked up the mail this morning."

Shelby squealed. "Is there something for Katy?"

Dad nodded.

A funny little tingle tiptoed up Katy's spine.

Shelby grabbed Katy's hands. "Hurry, Katy!"

Katy hurried. And she nearly fell off the cart.

Dad caught her arm and set her upright, shaking his head. He clicked his tongue on his teeth. "Better let me help Shelby. You might send her nose-first into the dirt."

Shelby waved her hands at Katy. "Go ahead. I'll catch up."

Katy took off for the house, her heart pounding. She careened into the kitchen and came to a panting halt. Rosemary looked up from rinsing radishes in the sink. Even before Katy asked, she nodded toward the table. "I put it in your spot."

Katy managed a quick smile and then she dashed to the table. She snatched up the letter, addressed to Miss Kathleen Lambright. She stared for a few seconds at the neat block printing, envisioning Jonathan's long, tapered fingers writing the letters of her name. A giggle rose in her throat.

Shelby limped into the room, her face alight with curiosity. "What's he say?"

Katy flattened the envelope against her chest with both palms. "I haven't opened it yet. I'm afraid to."

Rosemary chuckled, sending a crinkled smile across the kitchen. "Oh, Katy ..."

Shelby bopped Katy on the arm. "Get over it! I wanna see what it says!"

Katy gulped and lowered the envelope. With shaking fingers, she carefully peeled back the flap. "He said he isn't much of a writer. There might not be much here."

Shelby nearly bounced in place. "Just open the silly thing, wouldja?"

Rosemary's laughter rang.

Katy scowled at both of them and finally pulled a sheet of folded paper from the envelope. One sheet. And apparently with writing only on one side, because the part facing out was blank.

Shelby put her hand on her hip. "Katy, I'm gonna take that thing away if you don't hurry up."

"Okay, okay!" Katy sucked in her breath and held it while she slowly unfolded the sheet. Not only did it contain writing on only one side, the letter was only one sentence long. But when Katy read the sentence, she let out a squeal of delight.

Rosemary and Shelby both jumped.

Rosemary clamped her hand to her chest and exclaimed, "Katy! My word!"

Shelby held out her hands and wriggled her fingers. "What's it say? What's it say?"

Katy grinned and jammed the letter, writing out, toward Shelby.

Shelby read aloud, "Katy, I'll see you soon. Jonathan."

THE END

Discussion Questions for *Katy's Decision*

1. Shelby expected a fun summer with Katy—playing with the new foal, learning new things, and simply spending time talking and giggling with her best friend—but instead works most of the time in Rebecca's shop. If you were Shelby, how would you have reacted to the change in plans?

2. Katy and Caleb's relationship changes a lot in this book. What do you think might have happened between Katy and Caleb if Jonathan hadn't come to the community?

3. *Katy's Decision* takes place in Katy's comfort zone—Schellberg. Do you think you could live in Katy's community for several months? Was there anything about the customs that surprised you?

4. Was it fair of Katy's family to make her take responsibility for the fabric store all summer? Explain why.

5. Throughout the series, Katy dreams of becoming a writer. Do you think her job with the local paper will lead to bigger things? Why? What do you think Katy will do with her poetic side?

6. It appears Katy will be going to school in the fall, and she and Jonathan may be spending more time together. Do you think her upcoming school year will be easier than her sophomore year? Explain why. How do you think Bryce and Katy will interact once school starts, especially if Jonathan starts classes as well?

7. Do you think Katy's experiences in the secular world will change anything inside her sect? Would those changes be a good or a bad thing, in your opinion? Give reasons why.

8. With what you know about Katy's life, her dreams, and her Old Order Mennonite world, imagine Katy's future. (For instance, what will she be doing when she's eighteen?)

Talk It Up!

Want free books?
First looks at the best new fiction?
Awesome exclusive merchandise?

We want to hear from you!

Give us your opinions on titles, covers, and stories.
Join the Z Street Team.

Visit zstreetteam.zondervan.com/joinnow
to sign up today!

Also—Friend us on Facebook!

www.facebook.com/goodteenreads

- Video Trailers
- Connect with your favorite authors
- Sneak peeks at new releases
- Giveaways
- Fun discussions
- And much more!